KILLER
HEADLINE

**Center Point
Large Print**

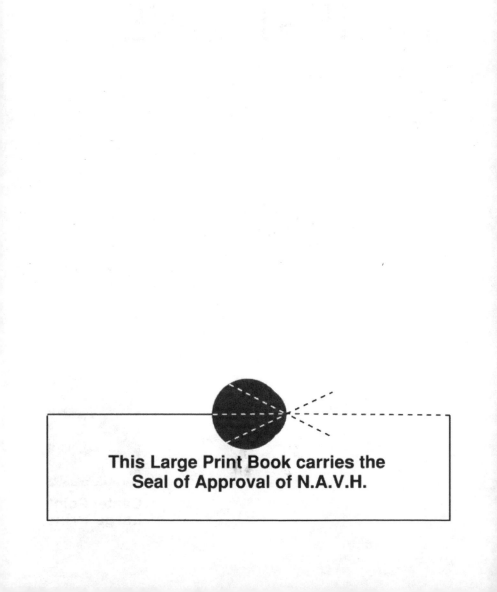

**This Large Print Book carries the
Seal of Approval of N.A.V.H.**

KILLER HEADLINE

Debby Giusti

CENTER POINT LARGE PRINT
THORNDIKE, MAINE

Special thanks and acknowledgment to Debby Giusti
for her contribution to the
Protecting the Witnesses miniseries.

This Center Point Large Print edition
is published in the year 2010 by arrangement with
Harlequin Books, S.A.

The text of this Large Print edition is unabridged.
In other aspects, this book may vary
from the original edition.
Printed in the United States of America.
Set in 16-point Times New Roman type.

ISBN: 978-1-60285-716-2

Library of Congress Cataloging-in-Publication Data

Giusti, Debby.
  Killer headline / Debby Giusti.
    p. cm.
  ISBN 978-1-60285-716-2 (library binding : alk. paper)
  1. Large type books. I. Title.
  PS3607.I73K55 2010
  813'.6—dc22
2009045405

To my precious family
For your love, support and encouragement

I lift up my eyes to the mountains:
From where shall come my help?
My help shall come from the Lord
Who made heaven and earth.

—*Psalms* 121:1-2

PROLOGUE

MEMO: TOP SECRET/TOP PRIORITY
To: FBI Organized Crime Division;
    U.S. Marshals Office
From: Jackson McGraw,
    Special Agent-in-Charge,
    Chicago Field Office,
    Federal Bureau of Investigation
Date: February 5, 2010
Re: Operation Black Veil

According to the FBI informant who wears a black veil and has recently come forward, the medical condition of the head of Chicago's Martino crime family, Salvatore Martino, continues to decline. The family's operation is now run by his son, Vincent Martino, currently out on bail and scheduled to stand trial for murder in June.

Activity within the family compound has increased significantly. Many of the major capos have visited Vincent at his Chicago home. Speculation on the street is that Vincent needs to prove himself to his father before the elder don dies. Whether the capos are paying allegiance to their new don or planning a change in their current operation is not known at this time.

The U.S. Marshals Office in Billings, Montana, notified the FBI concerning two women in Witness Protection murdered within the last month. Both had green eyes and ties to organized crime. Their deaths indicate growing Mafia activity in that state and may have been botched attempts to kill Eloise Hill, presumed to be in Montana. Hill has green eyes and testified against Salvatore Martino twenty-two years ago, resulting in his incarceration.

A Missoula news reporter contacted Detective Clay West, Chicago P.D., seeking information on the Martino family in reference to the murders. Action is now being taken to ensure the reporter focuses her interests elsewhere.

Law-enforcement personnel are instructed to notify SAC Jackson McGraw, FBI Chicago, with information pertinent to the Martino family, organized crime and/or the two murder cases.

ONE

Reporter Violet Kramer looked up from her laptop —relieved the drapes were drawn and the doors locked—as the car passed her house yet again. The sound of the souped-up engine and pounding bass cut through the otherwise still night.

A gang of rowdy troublemakers had moved into Missoula, prowling the streets and bringing a wave of crime that worried local residents, especially the older folks who lived in her neighborhood. Concerned though Violet was about the increased crime, her attention tonight was focused on her computer screen and the information she'd compiled over the last few weeks.

Violet could smell a good story, and this one was as strong as Limburger cheese. She just had to keep digging until she uncovered all the bits and pieces that would turn a good beginning into a great front-page spread, sure to improve her current odd-man-out status at the *Missoula Daily News*.

Even more important, the story would warn other women who might be in danger. Women who had somehow tangled with organized crime. Like Ruby Summers Maxwell and Carlie

Donald, both murdered in Montana. Both young and attractive with the dubious distinction of having testified against the mob.

Another interesting similarity, both women had green eyes. An important clue or coincidence? Violet wasn't sure.

She had little to go on concerning Ruby's death, except a funeral announcement and an e-mail from a reporter friend who worked on the local rag in the town where Ruby had been killed. The full story never appeared in print. Women in Witness Protection didn't make the headlines in the morning news.

Luckily, Violet's diligent search of area newspapers had paid off with a photo of Jade Summers—the very-much-alive twin sister of the murder victim—standing next to her beau, Deputy U.S. Marshal Micah McGraw. In the forefront of the picture sat swarms of preschoolers watching a clown at the library where Jade worked. The kids were cute, but Violet was only interested in the woman at the marshal's side. Slender frame, expressive eyes and a crown of russet hair that swept over her shoulders. At least now, Violet knew what Jade's murdered twin—Ruby Summers—had looked like.

Inserting her flash drive into her home laptop, Violet pulled up the file containing Carlie Donald's autopsy report—acquired through another contact.

. . . remains of a slender female . . . cause of death strangulation . . . abrasions and con-tusions of the anterior neck . . . no foreign materials evident beneath the fingernails . . . graphite noted on the right hand . . . froth in the trachea and bronchi . . .

Closing her eyes, Violet tried to block out the details playing through her mind. Her day had started early with a five-mile run before church. She had spent the afternoon working on the story, which had stretched the long day into an even longer night.

Right now, she needed to go to bed and forget about the two Mafia hits in-state since the New Year. And it was only February. Most folks believed bad luck came in threes. So, who would be the next to die?

Life was sacred, and those who preyed on the weak needed to be apprehended and brought to justice. If the police couldn't handle the job, Violet would.

Her cell rang. She glanced at her watch—twelve-fifteen—and reached for her phone, noting the caller's Chicago area code. "Kramer."

"It's Gwyn."

"I planned to check online in case you left a message," Violet said. The informant had told her never to phone lest her boyfriend—a mobster who worked with the Martino family—answer the call.

"Angelo's away for the night. I bought one of those nontraceable cell phones. Wanted you to know the latest."

Violet's stomach tightened, hearing the wariness in Gwyn's voice. "You're okay, aren't you?"

"Angelo's acting strange. He said everyone's on edge. Vincent Martino's making changes. Angelo knew where he stood when the old don, Salvatore, was in charge. With Vincent, things aren't so clear. Angelo said the new don has to prove himself to his father before Salvatore dies. Somehow it involves those women who were killed in Montana."

Just as long as Gwyn didn't get hurt.

Although Violet had never met her informant in person, she and Gwyn had connected online a little over a year ago when Violet had researched a possible story lead on the mob. She'd never completed the story, but the mobster's girlfriend had kept in touch, providing more and more insider information. With Violet's encouragement, Gwyn had recently admitted she wanted to make a new life for herself free from Angelo and the mob.

"Some of the capos are upset," Gwyn said. "Evidently, the hit men went after the wrong women."

"You mean, Ruby Summers Maxwell and Carlie Donald weren't supposed to die?"

"The target was someone else. A gal named

12

Eloise Hill. At least that's what Angelo heard. She testified against Salvatore years ago."

"And Vincent wants her dead to gain favor with his ailing father?"

"Vincent lacks Salvatore's charisma. Some say he's more interested in women than in running the organization."

"Can you find out more about Eloise for me? And let me know if any other women are being targeted?"

"I'll see what I can do." Pulling in a deep breath, Gwyn continued. "Remember Cameron Trimble, that sleazy pimp I told you about?"

"The guy who's in the hospital?"

"That's right. He'll be laid up awhile thanks to the undercover cop you know."

A rush of warmth fluttered over Violet's mid-section. "You mean, Clay West? We met a couple times, that's all."

"Whatever." Gwyn paused for a moment. "You called him, didn't you?"

"Three nights ago. I thought he'd tell me something new about the shake-up in the Martino family."

"Did you . . . ?" Gwyn's voice hitched. "Did you mention my name?"

"Of course not. I promised you the first time you contacted me that I'd never divulge your identity. I told Clay I'd heard his cover had been compromised, that's all."

"No one's upset about Cameron getting hurt. What they're upset about is your cop friend infiltrating a portion of the mob operation. Evidently, Clay West was after the guy who runs prostitution in the city. The cops had a sting planned that would have exposed him."

"So because Clay went after Cameron, the cops lost their opportunity and had to back off?"

"That's right. Now the mob's worried Cameron might talk. The family sent in one of their high-power lawyers who plans to have the pimp sue for damages. A concussion, three cracked ribs and a broken jaw constitute police brutality. At least that's the argument the lawyer will use."

Violet hated hearing about any law-enforcement officer shoving his weight around, but Clay West didn't seem the type to lose his cool. There had to be more to the story.

"What about that feature you're writing?" Gwyn asked. "You said it would be picked up by papers across the country. The mob would be forced to lay low for a while, which would give me a chance to make my break from Angelo."

"An overview of the story is on my editor's desk. I'm hoping he'll give me the go-ahead soon. As I've told you before, Gwyn, if there's any way I can help you, just let me know."

Once Gwyn had disconnected, Violet placed the phone back on the cradle. The main obstacle keeping the story from print would be her editor.

Stu was more interested in local news than what was happening in Chicago. Hopefully, the tie-in with two in-state murders would make the difference.

Three nights ago, Violet had called Clay, hoping he would provide additional information to beef up her submission. But instead of helping, he'd accused her of being an idealist. Not the worst name in the books but her spine had stiffened when he threw naive into the mix. *Déjà vu* of what he'd told her two years ago in Chicago.

Of course, back then, she *had* been naive and foolish. Closing down her computer, Violet smiled at her own audacity the night she'd stopped by the hole-in-the-wall Chicago bar and grill some of the Martino soldiers had been known to frequent. Luckily, God had been watching out for her.

Instead of the Mafia, she'd found Clay. Scruffy beard. Unkempt hair. Piercing black eyes. The guy in the corner had "don't mess with me" written all over him, along with rugged good looks that made him impossible to forget.

He'd stopped by her table long enough to warn her she was out of her element and to hightail it back to safer parts of the city. A hardcore Mafia-type wouldn't have worried about her safety. The concern she heard in his voice had said more than words.

Putting the investigational skills she'd learned

in journalism school to the test, she'd come upon an old photo of the graduating class at the Illinois Police Academy. The too-considerate mobster was none other than Detective Clay West.

Once she had a name, she learned he'd married young and divorced soon thereafter. His ex had died a few years later. The handsome cop fought crime with as much passion as Violet had searching the Internet for clues to the mob's corrupt control.

Realizing the wealth of information an undercover cop could provide if they teamed up, Violet had staked out the grill and tried to follow Clay home a few nights later. She'd lost him on the street, never suspecting he had doubled back. When he'd pulled her into a nearby alleyway and had given her a piece of his mind, she'd been hard-pressed to focus on his anger.

Standing way too close in the shadows, she'd noticed the scent of his leather jacket and the woodsy smell of his aftershave, as well as the tiny nick on the cleft of his chin. He'd tried to convince Violet she was in way over her head and getting into his business could cause problems for both of them.

Despite his raw appeal that had caused her heart to trip along her rib cage, the story came first. Violet had ignored his warning and planned to dig deeper into the mob's activities. All that ended a few days later when the permanent position she had hoped to land at the *Gazette* went to another intern. With no other journalism openings in the Windy City, Violet had accepted a position on the *Missoula Daily News*, where she'd languished for the last two years.

Fast-forward to a few days ago when Gwyn had mentioned an undercover cop named Clay West. Since Violet and the cop had a history of sorts, she had phoned him, hoping he'd provide more information about the murders in Montana. Clay's terse responses to her probing questions confirmed calling him had been a big mistake.

Monday morning, Violet was still thinking about her Mafia story as she stood at the end of her editor's desk, listening to Stu Nelson lecture her about staying on task. As much as Violet wanted to set Stu straight, she needed to pick her battles.

Keep the editor happy.

Violet had imprinted those words on her brain in Chicago. She was a good writer. Stu had said as much on more than one occasion. But he refused to assign her the hard-hitting features she wanted to write. Two years on staff and she continued to get the fillers and fluff stories.

Anyone could pull together a litany of facts and feed them to the readers. Violet's strength was finding the story within the story. She prided herself on going deeper, thinking bolder, writing stronger than anyone else on staff. And that wasn't egotism. It was fact.

A fact her editor didn't seem to realize.

"The number of cops on the force has decreased while crime is on the rise," Stu continued, his slightly this-side-of-sixty face wrinkling like a prune. "That's the story I wanted you to write. Not your biased opinion of the chief of police." Stu wagged his finger close to her face for emphasis.

Aware of the office door hanging open, Violet knew her peers had overheard his lambasting.

"Did you happen to look at the information I typed up concerning the two murders?" Violet threw the question into the mix.

Stu raised his brow, and his finger returned to the aforementioned position. "There you go again, chasing windmills. The fact that two women died on opposite ends of Montana has no correlation to anything you think might be happening in Chicago, Illinois."

"The mob exists, Stu."

"Maybe in Chicago, but we're over twelve-hundred miles away. If you change the slant of a story I assign again, you can head back to Chicago. As I recall, the *Gazette* didn't ask you to stay on staff."

Oh, yeah, Stu was on a roll and had just gone in for the kill. "It was an internship after college," she offered in self-defense. "There was never any promise of permanent employment following the nine-month training period."

Backing her way to the door, she grabbed the knob, and when Stu waved her off, she slipped out of his office, feeling as if she'd just missed a head-on collision with a tractor trailer on Interstate 90.

Her heels clipped across the tiled floor. Quinn Smith looked up from his computer as she passed his cubicle and gave her a thumbs-up. "Keep the faith, Violet."

She tried to smile back at one of the *Missoula Daily News*'s lead reporters. Medium height but athletic for a midfifties guy with a receding hairline, Quinn seemed to understand how she ticked.

Violet threaded her way across the length of the newsroom to her small desk, tucked along the far wall. One of the realities of her position was her distance from the editor's office.

Out of sight, out of mind.

Stu would see her in a more favorable light after she turned in the completed story that tied the Chicago crime family with the two women who had died in Montana.

A story he had just rejected, her voice of reason cautioned. Advice she chose to ignore.

She slipped behind her desk, into the swivel chair that had lost its swivel probably last century, kicked off her shoes and logged on to a Web site she'd created in college.

A lone partition separated her desk from the main hallway leading to the elevators where Jimmy Baker now stood, peering down at her. Gangly tall with a school-boy smile, the junior reporter was a friend from her University-of-Montana days.

"Sounded bad." He smiled with encouragement as he rounded the partition and sidled up behind her desk.

She lowered her voice so only he could hear. "FYI, I'm on to something big."

"Ah, Violet, you're gonna get into trouble. I can feel it coming."

"Not if the story increases subscriptions and establishes the *Daily News* as the number-one rag in Montana."

"Before success goes to your head, check your voice mail. Your phone rang off the hook while you were in with Stu."

Violet pulled the receiver to her ear and punched the message button.

He had her at hello.

No mistaking Clay West's voice or the ripple of excitement that tingled down her neck. Something about the way he enunciated each syllable clearly and distinctly sent a mental five-by-seven glossy to hang in the recesses of her brain. Tall, dark and dangerous was the image that came to mind.

Now, here he was on her answering machine,

saying they needed to talk. Not once, but three times. If the man had any fault, likely it was impatience.

Jimmy peeked over her shoulder at her computer screen. "Good grief, Violet, is that the same Web site from our college days?"

She minimized the page, but that didn't stop Jimmy.

"After all this time, do you seriously think someone will come forward with information about your Aunt Lettie's murder? Weren't you six when she died?"

"I was seven," Violet corrected. So young, yet she still felt responsible for her aunt's death. If only she'd had the courage to run after her that night, Lettie might still be alive. Instead, fear had overpowered Violet. She'd returned to the security of her home and had never seen her aunt alive again.

"The cops couldn't find the killer. Doubtful you'll have better luck." Tenacious to a fault, he did the math on his fingers. "It's been what? Eighteen years?"

"Jimmy, let it go."

He leaned close to her ear. "I will if you stop with the Mafia story. I heard what Stu said. You're doing it again, Vi. Stepping on toes. Going against authority. It could cost you your job."

"Would you please back off?" Even friendship

had boundaries and recently Jimmy was stepping a little too close to the line.

Her phone rang. She pulled the receiver to her ear. "Kramer."

"Violet, it's Clay West. I was wondering if we could talk, perhaps this evening. I'm not sure you understood the urgency of what I told you the other night when you called. You're getting involved in something you shouldn't be. We could discuss it over—"

Violet looked up at Jimmy, who failed to get the message to back off. As much as she wanted to talk to Clay, she didn't need to listen to a third lecture in one day. Especially with Jimmy hovering close by.

"I'm afraid this isn't a good time."

"Yes, but—"

"I'll call you back."

Violet disconnected and glared up at the guy who refused to take a hint. "Goodbye, Jimmy."

"Later." Turning on his heel, he sauntered back to his desk that sat five rows closer to Stu's office.

Violet groaned. Because of Jimmy, she'd hung up on the very person who could provide information about the Martino family.

She made a mental note to call Clay as soon as she got home from work. Maybe they could smooth out the rough edges of their rather tenuous relationship. She'd enjoy being on firmer footing with the handsome and mysterious cop.

Violet transferred data for the revised article Stu wanted on the local police department on to her flash drive, as well as the information she'd compiled on the murdered women in Witness Protection.

Pulling her coat tight, Violet left the Plaza Complex hours later and made her way to the now-empty parking deck, her breath hanging in the frosty February air. Her car sat in the last row, farthest from the door, another sign of her standing at the *Daily News*.

She slid behind the wheel of her Mini Cooper, exited on to the main thoroughfare and snaked her way across town to the older neighborhood where she lived.

A crescent moon hung in the night sky, casting a band of light over the mountains that wrapped around the city. The stark beauty of God's creation wasn't lost on her this night despite the lousy day she'd had at the paper. Violet loved Montana's fertile valleys and snow-covered mountaintops. Perhaps God had known what she'd needed two years ago when she failed to land the job at the *Gazette*. Undoubtedly, He was guiding her path even now. Hopefully, something good would come from all her hard work.

Please, God, make it happen.

Turning on to her street, Violet angled into the

alleyway and parked in the freestanding garage situated at the rear of her property.

Leaving the warmth of the car, she tugged the coat collar up around her neck and hastened along the cement walk to the mailbox out front.

Glancing up and down the empty street, Violet grabbed the stack of bills and shivered, not from the cold but from an immediate sense of foreboding. Usually she had nerves of steel. Tonight her steel had turned to rubber.

She clutched the mail tightly in her hand, mildly comforted by the rhythm of her footfalls along the sidewalk, as if the sound could spook away the unwelcome and unwanted sliver of concern that shimmied down her spine.

Moonlight spilled over the rear of the house, but the front remained cloaked in darkness. Stopping short at the bottom of the porch steps, Violet noticed for the first time how the windowpanes, huge squares of opaque blackness, stared back at her like faceless gargoyles, taunting her for her foolish fear.

She should have left on a light.

A stiff wind blew at Violet's back, causing her hair to billow around her face. She yanked the flyaway strands into submission and climbed the stairs.

The sound of a car engine broke the silence. Headlights turned on to her street. Violet's neck tingled a warning.

She jammed her key into the lock then glanced back as the car slowed. The driver's face, hidden in shadow, stared in her direction.

Violet turned the key, seeking the protection of her home. The door inched open, and she slipped into the dark interior.

A floorboard creaked. She glanced toward the kitchen.

A hooded, bulky form stood backlit in moonlight.

Violet screamed.

The man opened the back door and disappeared into the night.

Heart pounding like a snare drum, Violet dug for the cell phone in her purse. Her fingers trembled as she clutched the cold metal. Before she tapped in 911, a rustling sounded on the porch behind her.

Warm breath fanned her neck and a hand touched her shoulder.

Violet pivoted, ready to strike, and screamed once again.

TWO

"Violet, it's Clay West."

She stared at him, her eyes wide, limbs shaking.

"What happened?" he asked.

She gasped for air. "A man. In my kitchen. He ran out the back door."

"Call the cops. Stay inside. Lock your doors."

Clay raced through the house and out the kitchen door. A dog barked.

Searching the darkness, he saw movement in the distance and raced into the alleyway. A fleeing figure turned on to the main road.

Clay ran to the corner. The guy climbed into a late-model SUV, dark paint job, parked along the side of the road and drove away. Clay stood for a long moment watching the vehicle disappear then, hurrying back to Violet's house, he tapped on the kitchen door.

"It's Clay. Open up, Violet."

She inched the door open and peered out at him from the shadows. Eyes wary, face drawn. His heart went out to her. For all her bravado, she looked scared to death.

"I called 911," she said. "The police are on their way."

As if in response, a siren sounded in the distance.

"Did you see the guy?" Clay stepped inside and locked the door behind him.

"Not his face."

Clay glanced around the kitchen. Nothing seemed out of place. Moving into the living room, he flipped on the overhead light.

The home was an eclectic assortment of mix-and-match furnishings. Comfy and cozy. Bright colors, soft pillows and knock-off artwork blended into a warm and inviting atmosphere he instantly liked. A desk in the far corner held a laptop, table lamp, phone and an assortment of papers.

Violet wrapped her arms around her waist. The color had drained from her pretty face. She raised a hand to her throat, her breath ragged.

"What . . . what are you doing here?" she asked.

As much as he wanted to reassure her, she needed the truth. "The FBI in Chicago feel you're in danger. Special Agent-in-Charge Jackson McGraw asked me to pay you a visit. You've been digging into Mafia business, Violet. The mob silences anyone who comes too close."

Her brows rose. "This wasn't the mob. A bad element's moved into the city. This was local, Clay."

"And you came to that conclusion because—?"

"Because the intruder fled. The mob would have killed me."

A visual flashed through Clay's mind. He envisioned her bound and gagged with a gun to her head. Swallowing the bile that instantly filled his throat, Clay blinked twice, relieved to find a flesh-and-blood and very much unharmed Violet standing in front of him.

"You can't be sure it wasn't the mob." Clay noted her drawn drapes, needing to turn his focus back to security issues instead of the way his pulse quickened whenever he was near her. "Are all your windows and doors locked?"

"Of course." Then she hesitated. "Except in the laundry room."

Violet stepped into the hallway and opened the door to a small room containing a washer and dryer. "I keep the window open to let out the hot air from the dryer."

Just as she'd said, the window was open and the screen unattached. "Don't touch anything. We'll let the cops check it out. That might be the way the guy broke in."

The siren neared. Clay and Violet returned to the living area. He opened the door. A beefy cop, short hair, wearing a bulletproof vest and named O'Reilly shook his hand and then Violet's.

Clay explained he worked for Chicago P.D. and quickly detailed what had happened. After O'Reilly checked the house, he and Clay walked outside. Shining a flashlight around the laundry-room window and ground below, they found no

28

evidence to prove or disprove the window was the point of entry.

Following the cop's suggestion, Violet did a quick search of her valuables. Nothing seemed to have been disturbed.

The officer took Violet's statement while Clay stood to the side, his attention focused on the pretty reporter. Everything he remembered about Violet had been true. She was fresh and young and beautiful and full of life and unaware of the effect she had on him.

Two years ago, he'd picked her out in the crowd at the Chicago bar and grill and known immediately the low-rent dive wasn't the place for her dimples and curls and curves and the angora sweater that had hugged her body and made him want to wrap her protectively in his arms.

He still wanted to protect her. That's why he'd been on the road for the last forty-eight hours on special assignment from the Chicago FBI.

Pay Violet Kramer a personal visit so she gets the message to back off, Jackson McGraw had told him. Violet had made too many inquiries into the Chicago mob's activities. Bottom line, according to Jackson, she needed to stop investigating the Martino crime family and allow law enforcement to do their jobs.

Clay had tried to make that perfectly clear three nights ago when he'd received her unexpected phone call requesting information about the murdered women in Witness Protection.

Somehow, Violet had pieced together bits of information about two seemingly random crimes in Montana and deduced the Mafia's involvement.

She had beeped a warning on the FBI's radar, and if they knew about her inquiries, the Mafia did, as well. Wouldn't take long for organized crime to put a strangle hold on Violet Kramer—literally.

Clay's job was to get to her first.

Finished with his paperwork, Officer O'Reilly handed a business card to Violet. "Keep that laundry-room window locked, and if you remember anything else, give me a call. You heard cars driving up and down the street. Someone's been casing the neighborhood, but the intruder never expected you to walk in on him tonight."

O'Reilly nodded to Clay. "Having you in pursuit probably scared him, as well. Doubtful he'll hit this house again."

Violet and Clay thanked the officer and walked him to the door. Once he drove off in his patrol car, Clay checked his watch. He still had a job to do.

"I know it's late, Violet, but we need to go over some security measures you can take to protect yourself." He pointed to the table lamps. "Leave a light on so you don't come home from work to a dark house. Install dead bolts on your front and back doors. Lock all windows, even the one in the laundry room."

She nodded, her mouth pursed. "I won't leave it open again."

He glanced at the phone on her desk. "Call home before you pull into the garage. If someone's inside, the sound of the phone might encourage them to flee."

She squared her shoulders. "I can take care of myself, Clay."

He smiled at her flair of independence. "Seems to me you weren't quite so confident about an hour ago when the guy was standing in your kitchen. Just as I mentioned earlier, it could have been the mob."

"Could have, but wasn't. The officer agreed with me. It was local riffraff."

"In either case, don't leave your notes on organized crime where someone can read them." He pointed to the desk where her laptop sat, along with a stack of papers. The notes on top chronicled some of the Martino family's most recent exploits, which he'd noticed when Violet was occupied with the cop.

She dropped her hands to her hips. "You have no right to rifle through my papers."

Seems she was feeling a bit more confident now.

Violet cocked her hip. "Don't tell me you drove over twelve hundred miles just to give me a security briefing."

"I had a few days off and planned to take you out to dinner so we could discuss your security face-to-face." He kept his voice calm. She had been through a lot this evening. He needed to cut her some slack.

"You're probably hungry," Clay said. "We can discuss how you're going to stop gathering information on the mob over Chinese or Mexican. Maybe Thai?"

Anger flashed from her eyes. "You can't tell me what to do, Clay."

"For your own safety."

"The mob isn't the problem right now. You are." Her voice was razor sharp.

"You're upset," he said. "Surely once you've eaten—"

"Leave now or I'll call Officer O'Reilly and tell him I have another problem."

"Violet, you're acting irrational."

He should have weighed his words.

She pointed to the door. "Goodbye, Clay."

Things had certainly taken a turn for the worse. As much as he regretted upsetting her, Violet needed to realize her own vulnerability.

If a local punk could break and enter, the mob could, as well. Only they would have ensured she got the message to back off loud and clear, and their way of handling problems was usually fatal.

Hopefully, once Violet had time to process everything that had happened, she'd realize Clay's advice was sound. He had made his point. One she'd remember. Better to leave while he was ahead.

"I'll let myself out." Clay headed for the kitchen door. The cold night air swirled around him when he stepped outside. A scrap of paper blew along the walkway. Clay bent to retrieve the note he hadn't noticed earlier.

He unfolded the paper and read the typed message. *Back off!*

Had the man who'd broken into Violet's house intended to leave the warning? Violet's scream had frightened him, and the paper had probably fallen from his hand as he ran away.

The Mafia didn't usually warn its victims, yet someone in Missoula knew Violet's curiosity was taking her in a dangerous direction.

Was the mob using someone local to put the heat on Violet? If so, they wouldn't let up until she was quieted once and for all.

Clay glanced at her home. The light from her kitchen window spilled into the darkness. He wouldn't disturb her again tonight. Tomorrow would be soon enough.

His first duty was to convince Violet to stop digging around in Mafia business. The second was to learn where and how she got her information. The third was to ensure her safety. If the mob showed up in Missoula, he'd add a fourth bullet to the list.

Keep Violet alive.

Violet locked the door behind Clay, feeling relieved to have him out of her home. But when she looked at the spot where the intruder had stood, she wished she hadn't been so hasty sending Clay away. He offered security and a voice of reason. She regretted her outburst. Of course, she wasn't thinking clearly.

Having her home broken into had thrown her usual levelheaded composure into a tailspin. Clay's insistence on turning her misfortune into a teaching moment had rubbed her already stretched nerves to the point of breaking.

Peeved as she was at Clay, she knew he was right. Her inquiries about the mob could be her downfall if the Martino family found out. She needed to be careful.

Violet rechecked her front and back doors to ensure they were locked. As an added precaution, she wedged a straight-back kitchen chair under each doorknob to provide another obstacle should tonight's mystery guest return or Clay's warning about the mob prove true.

What had brought him to Missoula? Something more than her phone call the other night. The big guns in Chicago wouldn't have sent Clay on a wild goose chase to Missoula if she hadn't ruffled a few feathers in Illinois or stepped on someone's toes.

Her dark mood brightened. A knowing smile slipped across her lips. Score one for the home team.

Not bad, Vi. Not bad at all.

Officer O'Reilly had assured her tonight's intruder wouldn't be back, which was a relief. In addition, Clay's warnings wouldn't change her mind.

The undercover cop from Chicago hadn't scared her off. In fact, he'd made her more convinced than ever to continue the course she was on. She must have uncovered something that the cops and the Feds didn't want exposed. This story about the mob could be bigger than even she had expected.

Kicking off her heels, Violet settled into her desk chair and booted up her computer. She pulled up her e-mail and started a new message.

Her cursor followed each keystroke as she typed in Gwyn's address and *Need more info* as the subject line. In the message box, she typed, *Tell me everything you know about Clay West.*

"Thank you, Clay," she mumbled. "If it hadn't been for you, I might have given up on this story about women killed by the mob."

But nothing, not even a handsome cop, would stop her now.

●●●

Clay hustled down the dark street to where he'd parked his car. Sliding behind the wheel, he pulled his cell phone from his pocket and called Chicago.

FBI Special Agent-in-Charge Jackson McGraw answered on the second ring.

"Someone broke into the reporter's home. I chased the guy a couple blocks but lost him."

"One of Martino's guys?"

"The cops suspect locals. They've had a number of recent petty crimes in the area." Clay told Jackson about following the perpetrator, and the note Clay found when he left Violet's house later that night. "Doubtful the mob would have left a warning message. But they may have alerted someone local to keep her under watch. If the guy's being strong-armed to do the mob's bidding, he may have thought scaring Violet off would work to his advantage."

"Which is exactly what we're trying to do, as well."

"I drove home the point about her security issues. In fact, I conducted a little training exercise within the home as you requested."

Jackson chuckled. "Let me guess. Violet wasn't impressed."

"*Irritated* would be a better word to use."

"You pushed hard, eh?"

"Which seems to be my modus operandi." Clay

thought of the hot water he'd landed in recently. "I'm not convinced she's willing to back off."

"Ms. Kramer has a history of charging headlong into situations without weighing the consequences. At least that's what I picked up from a friend on the *Chicago Gazette*."

"I got the same story before I left town. Someone who works with the internship program filled me in. The woman knows no fear."

Clay thought of Violet standing in her living room. His presence had startled her, yet she'd recovered faster than most. Later, after the danger had passed and the cop had left, she'd pulled an extra layer of attitude around her slender shoulders. When that hadn't worked, she'd let her temper get the best of her. Through it all, she'd put up a tough defense.

"I've got a motel room for the night located near the highway coming into town. I'll spend tonight watching her house in case the guy decides to come back." Clay glanced at the modest but comfortable homes lining the street. "Tomorrow, I'll look for a place closer in. If I stay a few days, I can keep an eye on her and find out what she knows. Remember the old adage about never underestimate the enemy?"

"From the sound of your voice, I take it the woman got under your skin."

Clay straightened and squared his shoulders. "Absolutely not."

"Just make sure she understands the mob plays for keeps."

"Anything new on your end?" Clay asked.

"We've had additional confirmation the two women's deaths were tied with the Martino family. No news about Eloise. If we can't trace her, I'm praying the mob can't, either."

"I'd feel better if you knew she was safe," Clay said.

"Micah's helping us."

"Convenient to have a brother who's a Deputy U.S. Marshal in Montana."

Jackson chuckled again. "Unless sibling rivalry gets in the way."

Clay wouldn't know. No siblings, no parents, no wife or ex-wife, for that matter. Family reunions were a one-man show.

"Remember the baby Eloise gave up for adoption?" the agent asked.

"Of course, I remember Kristin. You arranged for her to be adopted by a family named Perry. He was a lawyer from Billings."

Jackson was silent for a moment. When he spoke, his voice was cold. "How do you know that information?"

Clay let out a lungful of air. "Look, Jackson. Eloise was important to me. Like family. I wanted to ensure the child's life wouldn't be tainted by the mob. You did everything by the book."

"Hopefully the mob wasn't as determined as you were to track her down."

"Hasn't Kristin been safe all these years?"

"Yeah, you're right. But her adoptive parents died recently, and she's trying to find her birth mother. Kristin paid Micah a visit not long ago."

Clay thought of Violet. "So another woman's sticking her nose where she shouldn't?"

"Exactly. Micah told Kristin to go home and let the Marshals find Eloise."

"I hope Kristin's not as headstrong as our friend the reporter."

"There's another complication. The Billings newspaper ran an article on Mr. and Mrs. Perry, including a color photo of the family. Kristin looks like her mom, green eyes and all."

"You think the Martino family might see the article?"

"Anything's possible."

"What's your brother say?"

"Micah's convinced the Marshals can find Eloise. Although his main interest recently has been another woman. Seems my dear brother's fallen in love. You heard about Ruby Summers Maxwell?"

"The woman in Witness Protection murdered last month?"

"That's right. Micah met her twin sister, Jade, while he was investigating the crime. One thing led to another. Now they're talking marriage."

"Which should be good news. How come I hear frustration in your voice, Jackson?"

When the FBI agent failed to respond, Clay filled in the blanks. "Has to do with Eloise, doesn't it?"

Jackson inhaled sharply. "She was long ago, Clay. A man has to move on."

"But you haven't."

"I still think about her."

"Doubtful I could have survived the Southside Foster Home without Eloise. You would have thought I was her long-lost kid brother the way she showed me the ropes and made me feel included."

Not that Eloise hadn't made her own mistakes. She'd given her heart to the wrong guy, gotten pregnant and ended up witnessing Salvatore Martino shoot two men in cold blood. One of the victims had been the father of her child. Jackson had been the rookie agent assigned to her case.

Although he rarely talked about his feelings, Jackson had fallen in love with Eloise. His job demanded he place her in the Witness Protection Program, which meant he'd never see her again.

"Keep me updated on your progress with Ms. Kramer," Jackson said. "And watch your back. After what happened to Cameron Trimble, I'm sure you're not on the Martino family's list of favorite people. I wouldn't want a supposed get-away trip to Missoula, Montana, to cost Chicago P.D. one of their finest officers."

Clay appreciated Jackson's support. Especially when his future on the force still hung in the balance.

"Thanks for going to bat for me."

"Cameron was a brazen punk who deserved what he got."

"Unfortunately, the inquiry board may not see it the way you do."

"They know you've been under a lot of pressure working undercover, Clay. Coming face-to-face with Trimble put you over the edge."

"A mistake I shouldn't have made."

"The chief said a road trip would do you good. 'Blow off steam' were his exact words. That was after I explained the inquisitive Violet Kramer needed to be stopped. Since she called you the other night demanding information on the mob, you're our go-to guy. Plus, you've got a history with her."

"We had a couple run-ins in Chicago, nothing more."

"Okay, but she knows you. That helps. Call me if you find out anything new. When people push hard there's usually a reason."

Clay thought of Eloise, who had been forced into Witness Protection, and Sylvia, who had turned her back on their marriage. He had lost both of them, but that was the past, and he needed to focus on the present.

Currently, his number-one priority was ensuring Violet Kramer didn't get hurt. Maybe he needed to change tactics. If he worked with her, she might let down her guard and tell him what she knew about the Martino family and the Montana murders.

Some duties were easier than others. Hopefully, getting close to the feisty Ms. Kramer would be a piece of cake.

THREE

Clay wasn't as convinced as Officer O'Reilly had been about tonight's perpetrator running scared. If the guy took orders from the mob, he'd be back. This time, Clay would be waiting.

He parked down the street from Violet's house where he had a full view of her property, including the garage in back of the house and a portion of the surrounding yard.

Violet turned on the rear flood lighting before the house lights flipped off.

"Sleep well, honey," he whispered.

The backyard was swathed in brightness, which should deter anyone approaching from the alley. The night was still, and the sound of a car engine would travel in the frigid air. Clay's mind wandered as the hours passed. He thought back to the foster home and Eloise who had tried to talk him into accepting Christ into his life.

He'd taken the first steps and had become somewhat comfortable dialoguing with the Man upstairs until Eloise's situation had taken a negative spin. Didn't take long for Clay to reconsider his opinion of the Lord.

A few bad choices only compounded Clay's feeling of alienation. Married too young and divorced before he knew what being a husband was all about added to his hesitancy to depend on anyone, even God.

Now he faced at least two more weeks of probation until the board of inquiry made their decision. "Slam dunk," most of the guys on the force had said, slapping his back and praising him for the way he'd handled Cameron.

Not what they would have done, of course. But then none of them had an ex-wife who had been pimped and mainlined with heroin until she didn't know the difference between right or wrong.

Clay let out a frustrated breath.

After all that had happened, Jackson's request had surprised Clay almost as much as hearing Violet's voice the other night. Hard to imagine the FBI would want him to pay the sassy reporter a visit and that Chicago P.D. would let Clay go. Of course, every law-enforcement officer in the Windy City knew Special Agent-in-Charge Jackson McGraw usually got what he wanted.

Clay's cell phone chirped. He flipped it open, read the caller ID and smiled. "I was just thinking about you."

Jackson chuckled.

"What's up?"

"I contacted the local chief of police after your last call. His name's Walter Howard. Wanted him to know you were in town."

"Did you mention Violet?"

"He knows her. They're from the same hometown. I told him we were concerned the Mafia might be spreading its muscle into his neck of the woods."

"Which probably caught his interest."

"He said he didn't need or want any more trouble. Seems the local P.D. has a retention problem. Slots vacated by older officers who've retired haven't been filled. Younger guys sign on for a few years then transfer to better-paying lines of work. He's understaffed and worried."

"Sounds typical of a lot of areas of the country."

"Despite the low recruitment, the chief said to call if you need anything. He sounds competent. Don't hesitate to contact him, Clay."

"What about the Martino family?"

"More activity at their compound. Change is definitely in the air. Just wish we had a better handle on how it'll go down."

"Might be time to put a task force together."

Jackson's silence was telling.

"Okay. I get the picture." Clay smiled. "You've already got one in place, right?"

"Just proves, we think alike. I haven't mentioned it before, but there's a safe house in the local area. Worst case scenario, of course. Just keep her safe. I don't want another woman killed in Montana."

Clay flipped his cell closed, the gravity of Jackson's statement hung heavy on his shoulders. Clay had a job to do no matter how attractive Ms. Kramer happened to be.

The sound of a car engine caught his attention. Clay trained his eyes on the road ahead. Headlights approached from a distance.

The car swerved as it rounded the corner. A late-model SUV. The vehicle made a large swath around Clay's car then pulled to a stop at the far corner. The driver cut the engine.

The door opened, and a man dropped to the pavement. Illuminated for a moment by the interior lighting, Clay made note of the guy's jeans, dark sweatshirt zipped over his chest and a beanie pulled low over his hair. He appeared close in height to the man Clay had chased earlier. Could he be the same guy, returning to drive home the point he'd tried to make with Violet?

The man eased the driver's door closed then glanced at the row of houses, his gaze lingering longer on Violet's home than the other modest dwellings on the street.

Clay's gut tightened.

Beanie-man headed for the shadows. The guy was definitely up to no good.

Clay grabbed his cell and placed a call to

police headquarters. The dispatcher said she'd notify a cruiser in the area.

Silent as a cat, Clay crawled from his car and grabbed the guy from behind.

"What the—" the punk groaned. He jerked but couldn't pull free from Clay's grasp.

He shoved him toward the street and slammed him against his car. "What are you doing?"

"Nothing, man." He appeared to be about eighteen or nineteen.

Clay tugged at his arms. "Don't lie to me, kid. What's your name and who are you working for?"

"Jamie . . . my name's Jamie Favor." He shook his head. "I don't work for no one."

A siren screamed in the distance. The sound grew louder. Flashing lights broke through the darkness as a cruiser turned on to the street and braked to a stop in front of Clay's car. O'Reilly got out just as a second police sedan approached from the opposite direction.

"Hey, man, I didn't do nothing wrong," the punk moaned.

"Did you plan to break into someone's house?" Clay demanded. "Frighten someone? Steal a few valuables?"

The kid shook his head. "No way."

"Got yourself a live one, eh, Clay?" Officer O'Reilly said as he neared.

Clay nodded toward the SUV. "The kid parked

down the block then headed this way. He hugged the houses, staying in the shadows."

"What are you doing, young man, this time of night?" O'Reilly asked.

"Visiting my girlfriend."

"She lives on this street?" The Missoula cop feigned surprise.

Jamie nodded. "I thought she did."

O'Reilly patted him down.

"Look what I found." He yanked an automatic from the punk's waistband.

"Ah, man," the punk lowered his head.

Pulling out handcuffs, the officer rattled off Jamie's Miranda rights then clicked the cuffs in place. "Let's get you down to headquarters, Jamie, and see what else you might want to tell us." O'Reilly passed the kid on to the second officer who herded Jamie into the backseat of the cop car.

Clay slapped O'Reilly's shoulder. "Thanks for getting here so fast."

"No problem. You think he's the guy who broke into 518 earlier?"

Clay followed the cop's gaze to Violet's house. "Hard to tell. Instinct tells me that first guy was bigger, but I didn't get close enough to know for sure. Find out if Jamie has ties with anyone in Chicago. The Mafia's caused some problems in Montana. The FBI suspects they're interested in someone in-state."

O'Reilly pursed his lips. "And the reporter? How's she play into the mix?"

"Ms. Kramer's a bit more inquisitive than she should be for her own good. The mob doesn't like anyone on their heels. She's gotten a little too close."

"I'll have the guys on patrol keep watch on this neighborhood. There's been rumor of someone dealing drugs a block over. Jamie may have been heading that way. If he talks, we may be able to close down the operation. Appreciate the help you provided tonight."

Clay gave the officer his cell-phone number. "Call me when you find out what the kid was doing."

"Roger that. Stop by headquarters later, if you've got time. I'll tell you what we learned."

Clay appreciated O'Reilly's invitation.

Two men up to no good in one night. Every cop knew coincidences didn't apply to law enforcement.

Trouble had found Violet Kramer twice. In Clay's opinion, that was two times too many.

He turned at the sound of a front door opening to see Violet step on to the porch. Her hair swirled around her oval face in tiny ringlets wound as tight as she seemed.

She wore jeans and a parka and a pair of hot pink, fuzzy bedroom slippers that slapped down the stairs and sidewalk as she stormed toward him.

"What in the world is going on, Clay? Sirens and flashing lights in the middle of the night? How can anyone sleep?"

She glanced at the crowd of neighbors, many of them senior citizens, who gathered on the opposite side of the street and were watching with interest. One sweet older lady waved. Violet smiled a greeting before she turned back to Clay, the smile gone.

He stepped toward her. Did the woman have no fear?

"Everything's under control, Violet. No need to worry. The police have the perpetrator. They'll get to the bottom of what he was doing on your street."

"And what was he doing, Clay?"

He heard the sharpness in her response. Probably due to the late hour or maybe the number of folks who were watching and wondering about her involvement in the drama.

"He appeared to be casing the neighborhood. Officer O'Reilly's checking on any ties he might have with Chicago and the mob."

"The mob?" She stared into the patrol car, squinting her eyes against the flashing light. "He looks like a kid."

"The mob isn't comprised of only old men. They recruit teens whenever they can."

Her mouth pursed as if she didn't appreciate condescension, then her expression softened.

"Have you been out here all night?"

He nodded, noting the confusion that instantly clouded her face.

She hugged her arms. "It's got to be below zero."

"Actually, it's a bit warmer. The weatherman on the radio mentioned five degrees above zero about an hour ago."

She let out a long sigh. "Then I should offer you my thanks."

"A cup of coffee would help."

She smiled and the night warmed.

"One cup and I promise I'll let you get back to sleep," he said.

"Come on, then." She turned about-face and slapped her slippers up the steps and into the house.

Clay followed, noting the scent of vanilla as she lit a candle on the coffee table and hurried toward the kitchen. Working quickly, she poured coffee into the basket of the dripmaker. The smell of fresh grounds mixed with the candle into a rich blend as he pulled a straight-backed chair from the table and slipped into the seat.

He eyed her makeshift attempt to secure her back door with one of the chairs. For all her external bravado, the earlier break-in had bothered her.

Violet placed cream and sugar on the table and poured two mugs with the hot brew.

"Thanks." He raised his mug and eyed her through the steam. Her lips were swollen with sleep and her cheeks puffy. Sitting across the table from her, Clay felt that Violet had lowered some of her earlier barriers.

"You think the second guy had ties to the mob?" she asked, her voice filled with question.

Clay shrugged. "Hard to say. But he didn't belong on this street. Plus, he was packing an automatic."

Her eyes widened. "A gun?"

"That's right. A gun."

She straightened her shoulders. "Missoula's had problems, Clay. A bad element has infiltrated the city, and the police are struggling to handle the increased crime."

"They responded both times we needed them tonight," he said in their defense.

"Well, it's been a problem."

"How's Stu feel about law enforcement in the city?"

"He thinks they're handling the situation the best they can, but—" She hesitated.

"But you don't?"

"I have a natural concern about the tactics they use."

"What kind of answer is that, Violet? You're either for the cops or you're not. Has there been graft or corruption?"

She shook her head.

"What about racial profiling?"

"No, nothing like that."

Sounded as if the main problem with law enforcement was Violet.

Clay took a sip of coffee, allowing the stillness to settle around them. "When I left you earlier, I saw a scrap of paper outside your back door."

She cocked her brow.

"The words *Back off* were typed on the note. The guy may have dropped it as he ran away."

"Wouldn't Officer O'Reilly have seen the paper when he was checking outside the house?"

"Easy enough to miss a scrap of paper."

She looked down and nodded. When she glanced back up at him, her face was pulled tight with concern. "So, you think the break-in was a warning from the Martino family?"

"They may have contacted someone local to put pressure on you. As I mentioned, Violet, my advice is to stop making any inquiries into mob activity. Lie low until things die down."

She shook her head. "I'm not going to be frightened off from doing my job."

"You've got to use some common sense. Let the FBI and the cops handle the mob. They'll bring the Martino family down, but it will take time and good investigative skills."

"Which you're saying I don't have?"

"Of course not." He wasn't getting anywhere tonight. He glanced at the wall clock. Four-fifteen.

Violet needed to crawl back into bed, and he needed to head over to police headquarters. He wanted to learn what O'Reilly found out about Jamie Favor. The cops would keep watch over Violet for the rest of the night. Besides, dawn would be here soon enough.

He placed the mug on the table and pushed back his chair. "Coffee hit the spot. Thanks." He glanced at the chair wedged against the doorknob. "As I said earlier, might be a good idea to have dead bolts installed."

"I will."

She followed him out and waved goodbye as he walked down the front steps. Violet Kramer was stubborn and from what she'd said tonight, evidently, she didn't like cops.

That didn't put him in good stead. He wasn't one to let things bother him. But for some reason, Violet's opinion was important.

Violet was still thinking about everything that had happened the next morning. A break-in and another man apprehended in her front yard. Were both incidences tied with the mob? Surely not, no matter how much Clay West tried to convince her they were.

The Chicago FBI wanted her out of the picture, and Clay was determined to scare her into backing down. He'd learn soon enough that she didn't scare easily.

Violet finished writing a short article on the Missoula Women's Circle and their philanthropic work, which Stu had requested last week. Hopefully, he'd find the information to his liking.

Task completed, she checked her old college Web site where she kept hoping someone would leave a comment with information on Aunt Lettie's long-ago murder. But just as always, that in-box remained empty. Violet opened her working e-mail and found it void, as well.

Her phone rang.

She pulled the receiver to her ear, wondering if she'd hear Clay's voice. Not that she was interested, of course.

"Hey, Vi, it's Ross Truett. I got my hands on that photo you requested. Should arrive in your e-mail momentarily."

She smiled. "I owe you."

"Let me buy you dinner and we'll call it even. I've got business in Missoula on Friday."

"Sounds great. Call me when you get to town." Violet hung up and drummed her fingertips on her desktop, waiting for the incoming e-mail.

Ross was a college friend from a moneyed family who had rapidly worked his way up to assistant editor of the *Yellowstone County Reader*. The young editor had everything going for him. At least that's what her mother would say. She'd also say how happy she'd be if Violet connected with Ross on a permanent basis.

Correction. Her mother would be thrilled. But as far as Violet was concerned, he wasn't Mr. Right.

Clay West came to mind.

Talk about Mr. Wrong.

Hopefully, he'd be heading back to Illinois in a few days. Cute as he was, the detective had a cocky, smug attitude. She'd teach him a lesson or two about trying to change a woman's mind when she had her course set. Once she had gathered enough evidence to complete the Mafia story, Clay would realize she played hardball.

Then she had another thought. What if she wasn't the reason Clay had come to Montana? What if law enforcement suspected a third woman would be murdered? Made sense they'd want their undercover cop in place when surveillance learned of an another impending Mafia hit in the Treasure State. Perhaps this time in Missoula. The cops and the Feds wouldn't want Violet snooping around for fear she'd interfere with their operation.

And the next victim? Shouldn't she be warned?

Clay would probably remind Violet she was in danger, too. But the Mafia hadn't found her yet. Despite what he had said.

The message from Ross appeared on her screen along with an attachment. His comments were almost identical to what he'd said over the phone. Dinner the next time he was in Missoula.

Attachment for your eyes only. Keep the photo under wraps.

Violet saved the file to her flash drive then glanced around the newsroom. The others—occupied in their own work areas—either chatted on their phones or had their eyes focused on their monitors.

Clicking on the attachment, she watched the photo unfold across her screen. A woman lay on the floor, her neck scraped and bruised. Death by strangulation was never pretty.

Carlie Donald. May she rest in peace.

Would there be a third victim? If so, God help her, as well.

FOUR

Violet spent the next few hours covering a fundraiser for a local charity event. She'd compiled the information Stu wanted but still needed quotes from the event chairman and other key figures. She'd been playing phone tag with them all morning.

Frustrated at her lack of progress, Violet logged on to her e-mail. A new message from Gwyn appeared in her in-box.

I tried to call you, but your cell went to voice mail. After talking to you on Sunday, I realized this might be the only time Angelo's out of town for a while. To throw him off, I told him my mother was sick and that I needed to fly home to Texas. Instead, I caught a flight to Spokane. I rented a car and arrived in Missoula about thirty minutes ago. Can we meet? I saw a coffee shop near the UMT campus. Favorite Grinds. I'll be there at 11:30 a.m. today.

A mix of surprise and excitement swept through Violet. She had wanted to help Gwyn, but never expected she'd come to Missoula. Leaving Angelo and the mob behind had taken courage.

Gwyn had told Violet about the two women in Witness Protection who had been murdered. Surely, she realized Angelo could follow her. No matter what she needed, Violet would do everything she could to support Gwyn's decision to change her life for the better.

Violet checked her watch. Eleven-ten. She needed to hurry. Reaching for her purse, Violet glanced up to find Jimmy staring over the top of her computer screen.

"Looks like you got a hit," he said.

She closed her e-mail. "Do we need to talk about personal privacy?"

He tilted his head and exaggerated a pout. "You never minded sharing information in college."

"College ended three years ago, Jimmy. Things have changed."

He stared at her before asking, "What happened with that detective from Chicago who kept calling yesterday?"

Violet had never mentioned where Clay was from. "How do you know he was from Chicago?"

Jimmy raised his brows. Guilt was written all over his face.

Frustration bubbled up in Violet. "You tapped into my voice mail?"

"Only because you were tied up. The phone kept ringing. I wanted to make sure it wasn't urgent in case I needed to rescue you."

First Clay, now Jimmy. Why did men think she couldn't take care of herself?

"You invaded my privacy," she was quick to point out.

"I'm worried about you, Vi. If you keep pushing your own agenda, Stu might cut you off for good. You said the story you're working on is big. Remember we're in Missoula, Montana. Your moment of glory ended with the internship in Chicago."

She couldn't believe what she was hearing. "Moment of glory?"

"You pushed hard to land that internship and sacrificed friendships to get there."

"What?"

"A number of us had input into that final article you submitted with your application."

"Your photos were the only things I used that weren't my original work, and I gave you full credit for each and every shot."

Jimmy closed his mouth and stared at her.

Realization hit Violet like a two-by-four. "You wanted the internship."

"I wasn't the only one."

"Did anyone else feel I acted unfairly?"

He didn't respond.

"Give me a name," she prodded.

"All right. Ross Truett. He was in the running."

Violet stood, pushed back her chair and grasped the edge of her desk. "I didn't take the internship from anyone. I earned it fair and square."

Throwing her purse over her shoulder and grabbing her coat, Violet closed down her computer, pulled out the flash drive and swished past Jimmy.

What he'd said stung her pride. She'd never done anything to undermine anyone else. In fact, she'd been elated when Jimmy received praise. Ross, too.

Violet shrugged into one arm of her coat while the other sleeve dangled down her back. The elevator opened.

The first face she saw stepping on to the third floor was handsome, clean-shaven and smiling with a Cheshire-cat grin.

"Violet, I was hoping we could talk."

"Clay?"

Stu was the next to disembark just as Quinn walked around the corner. His face clouded when he saw the traffic jam by the elevator.

Violet tried to capture her elusive coat sleeve, feeling like a worm writhing on the cement after a rain. Any minute now, she expected a size-twelve shoe to smash her underfoot.

Clay grabbed the edge of her coat and redirected her flailing arm into the opening. Her cheeks burned with embarrassment, but she was grateful for his help and made a feeble attempt at introductions.

Clay shook hands with Stu. "Good to meet you, sir."

The editor looked at Violet over the top of his bifocals when she mentioned Clay worked for the Chicago P.D. "Don't tell me you're interviewing him for that story I rejected yesterday?"

"Story?" She feigned surprise.

"About the women murdered by the mob?"

So Stu had been listening.

Clay continued to smile, which she didn't appreciate.

The cop might find her present situation amusing, but trying to untangle herself from the noose Stu had slipped around her neck wasn't a laughing matter.

"You're not digging up more information, are you?" Stu added, like icing to a cake that was already top-heavy and ready to crumble.

"No, sir." She glared at the detective, hoping he'd help her out of her predicament.

Clay gave her a women-can't-refuse-me wink she found especially annoying. "I thought we had a date for lunch."

"Not today." She glanced from Stu to Quinn, who had moved into the circle, and to Jimmy, who stood off to one side.

Behind them, the elevator doors remained open.

Undoubtedly, God was offering her a way out.

"Excuse me, gentlemen, but I have an appointment to keep."

Violet pushed through the men and entered the elevator just as the doors closed. She let out a deep breath, relieved to be free of all of them. Well, maybe not Quinn. He'd been an innocent bystander.

Stu, Jimmy and Clay, on the other hand, were people she never wanted to see again.

Clay ranked at the top of the list.

"I could use a little help here." Violet glanced toward the heavens as she braked for yet another red light.

Everything was working against her today.

Stu and Clay on the same elevator? Talk about bad timing.

Once again, her cheeks burned as the scene at the paper replayed in her mind. Undoubtedly, she'd looked like a bumbling fool, struggling to put on her coat, one arm in, one arm out, babbling introductions and making no sense at all.

True to character, Clay had kept that cool cop facade she found both intriguing and irritating. Why was his body language impossible to read?

Stu was the exact opposite. One glance at his face said it all. He thought she'd gone off the deep end again. So much for gaining the boss's confidence.

Jimmy would probably have a few pithy comments to lob her way the next time he hovered around her desk. The only thing she'd read in his expression was disappointment.

The coffee shop appeared on her left. A no-parking zone stretched to the corner. Traffic was heavy, and Violet inched through the intersection and found a place to park about thirty yards down on the right.

Thank you, Jesus, for small favors.

Keys and purse in hand, she hastened along the sidewalk to make the rendezvous. Even at this distance, she looked through the coffee-shop windows and spied a number of customers sipping specialty drinks at small circular tables. Others waited for orders at the counter.

As Violet paused at the crosswalk for the light to change, someone caught her eye. Pretty with long brown hair, furrowed brow. Could that be Gwyn?

The woman's eyes locked on something behind Violet. Her face twisted. She rose from the table, grabbed her purse and left her coffee.

Glancing over her shoulder, Violet saw nothing.

The woman hurried outside.

"Ma'am? Gwyn?" Violet called to her over the sound of the passing traffic.

Digging into her purse, Violet retrieved her cell, clicked on the camera mode and took a photo. The woman's face appeared on the tiny screen.

"Wait, Gwyn?"

Violet watched her blend into a crowd of college students. Once the light changed and Violet crossed the street, the group—including the fleeing woman—had disappeared from sight.

Violet stepped inside the shop, the robust smell of brewing coffee sailed around her. She studied the remaining customers. No one glanced her way.

After ordering a tall coffee, heavy cream and two sugars, she dug in her purse for her wallet.

"Coffee's on me," a deep voice said behind her.

She turned to find Clay standing too close. The crooked smile curling his lips did something to her equilibrium. She took a step back and reached for the coffee the barista held out to her.

"I can take care of myself, Clay."

"Sure you can, but humor me, okay?"

Dropping a ten on the counter, she jerked a thumb over her shoulder.

"This should cover whatever he orders." Ignoring Clay's protests, she walked to a table by the window.

He grabbed a black coffee and pulled out a chair across the table from her. "Who was that woman?"

"What woman?"

"Come on, Violet. Level with me. The woman

you were racing to meet. You took her picture with the camera on your cell phone."

Cops could be so annoying. "A friend."

"Do your friends always run away when they see you?" Again, that aggravating but loveable crooked smile.

She shrugged. "Some follow me wherever I go. Others run away. I've got strange friends."

"Thanks."

"For what?"

"For calling me a friend."

Her cheeks burned. "That's not what I meant."

"Oh?" He raised a brow and feigned sadness. "So, I'm not a friend?"

Violet sighed. "You do this on purpose."

"Do what?"

"Talk in circles. You enjoy twisting my words. We're not friends. We're acquaintances. Friends require knowing each other longer."

"We met two years ago."

"And haven't seen each other since. That makes us acquaintances."

"At least, it's a start." He raised his mug. "Here's to our friendship. May it develop into something more."

His playful mood disappeared, and he stared at her with such raw emotion that her stomach turned a cartwheel.

All around them people chatted, chairs moved, outside traffic lined the street, but Violet's attention was riveted solely on his eyes—eyes that were saying unspoken words that made her skin tingle.

Surely she wasn't reading him right.

Her fingers gripped the coffee mug. With effort, she pulled her gaze from his as the waitress brought two sandwich platters and dropped one in front of Violet. Clay accepted the second plate and thanked the waitress.

He smiled at Violet. "I thought you might like something to eat. Pastrami on rye sound okay?"

Her favorite, although she wouldn't tell him. Her mouth watered as she looked down at the plate. After the coffee in the middle of the night, she'd stayed awake for hours, finally falling asleep just minutes before her alarm went off. Snooze control had given her twenty minutes more in bed but forced her to race from the house without eating breakfast to keep from being late for work.

She lifted the sandwich to her mouth and closed her eyes, savoring the delectable flavors. "I didn't realize I was hungry," she confessed.

Violet reached for the mustard at the same time as Clay. Their hands collided. Heat warmed her cheeks. If only her body wouldn't give her away.

"Ladies first," he said, but his hand remained playfully on top of hers. He rubbed his finger over her skin.

Her blush deepened. No doubt, the entire upper half of her body was scarlet. Yet she didn't move, enjoying the way his finger stroked her flesh.

Food was the last thing on her mind at the moment.

"I plan to hang around for a few days, Violet. Maybe we could pool our information and work together?"

Exactly what she'd wanted when she'd called him just days ago.

"I don't want you to get hurt," he continued. "Maybe if I help shed light on what's been happening, you'll see law enforcement is handling the situation."

"Sharing information sounds good, Clay. Why don't you start by telling me about the mob's next target?"

He pulled his hand back and shrugged. "I don't have any information about a possible hit."

"Isn't that what brought you to Missoula?"

He sighed. "I told you. I'm here to talk some sense into you."

She dropped the sandwich to her plate and put her hands on her hips. "You mean, what I'm doing is so important that the Feds sent you on a two-day road trip to shut me up?"

"Ensure your safety is more like it, Violet."

"Because two women have died in Montana and another one is in the crosshairs of the mob."

She leaned across the table and lowered her voice. "Give me her name, Clay."

"Her name and an exclusive on the story?"

Now she was getting someplace.

"Her name will be Violet Kramer if you don't stop involving yourself in the mob's business."

She straightened and jammed her thumb against her chest. "Now you're saying there's a hit out on me?"

He let out a deep breath and shook his head. "You're amazing."

She smiled. "I'll take that as a compliment."

"Maybe *determined* would be a better word to use."

"Tell me who you *think* will be the next victim in Witness Protection?" she pushed.

"Violet, please."

"Green eyes? Between twenty-one and forty years of age? Attractive?"

He shoved the sandwich into his mouth and turned his gaze toward the traffic passing on the street.

Violet picked up her sandwich and took a bite. Why couldn't Clay be more forthright about why he was in Missoula? Before she could come up with a way to make him talk, he pointed across the street.

"Isn't that the guy who was hovering around you at the paper today?"

"Jimmy?" Violet followed Clay's gaze. Instead

of her old college friend, she saw Quinn Smith climb into his car. "He's probably covering a story in the area."

"How much do you know about the people you work with, Violet?"

"Meaning?"

"Meaning, I need a list of their names. Surely, Stu would provide the information. I'll have the FBI run a background check on the staff."

As if that wouldn't improve her odd-man-out status on the *Daily News*. "Don't do me any favors, okay?"

"Someone broke into your house, Violet. You can't be too careful."

"Yeah, but I have to work with these people. They might not appreciate their private information aired like dirty laundry."

"If they don't have anything to hide, there shouldn't be a problem."

Except there was a problem. Clay was jumping to the wrong conclusion and would pull innocent people into an investigation that would prove nothing. The *Daily News* staff was made up of hardworking folks who did their jobs and went home to their families. No one was involved with the Chicago Mafia. In fact, the longer she thought about Clay infringing on their privacy, the more irritated she became.

Violet grabbed her purse and scooted her chair. "I have to get back to work."

"How about dinner tonight?"

"I can't, Clay."

"Can't or won't?"

Maybe both, but she wouldn't let him in on the secret. "I have plans."

He stood as she walked away. She needed some space and time away from Clay. The reaction he had on her was too unsettling. Violet liked to be in control, and she felt anything but when she was around the cocky Chicago cop.

In her rearview mirror, Violet saw Clay follow her back to the office. Once she pulled into the parking deck, he drove past.

"Good riddance," she mumbled although only halfheartedly.

Riding the elevator to the third floor, she stepped into the hallway, rounded the partition and slipped behind her desk. She worked on fillers for the rest of the afternoon. By 6:00 p.m., only a handful of reporters were still at their desks.

Digging her cell out of her purse, Violet pulled up the photo she'd taken on the street, sent it to her computer and stared at the face of the woman she'd seen running from the coffee shop. Pretty, with high cheekbones and an expressive brow.

Footsteps sounded in the hallway. Violet closed the window and glanced at the partition. Quinn's strong nose and receding hairline came into view.

He startled. "Violet? Didn't expect to see you here this late."

She shrugged, feeling her cheeks heat as she recalled the last time they'd met. Thank you, Clay West.

"I'm catching up."

Quinn nodded knowingly. "Stu told me you're working on a police recruitment piece."

"Which needs to be rewritten."

"Editors demand perfection. But I've seen your work so I'm sure that wasn't the problem."

His words of encouragement bolstered her flagging confidence. If only Quinn were her boss.

"I know you're eager to take on something with a little more meat, but bide your time, Violet. Right now, Stu's a little top-heavy with writers. You've seen the stats. Folks are getting their news from the Internet. Subscriptions are down. The economy has problems. He's walking a tightrope, trying to keep the paper up and running and in the red. Stu has some tough decisions to make in the days ahead."

"You don't mean cut staff?"

"That's one option."

Violet swallowed. She needed this job.

Quinn leaned over her desk and patted her hand in a fatherly sort of way. "Just work hard and you'll be fine. Stu knows you're a strong writer."

Glancing over his shoulder, his eyes keyed on

Jimmy's desk. "Some others may be in a less advantageous position."

"Are you talking about Jimmy?" Her old friend needed his job as much as she did.

"I'm not mentioning names. But since you brought him up, Jimmy's work sometimes falls short. Plus, you've seen how he and Stu butt horns."

Actually, she hadn't seen anything of the kind, but her desk was in the far rear corner. No telling what happened in the upper-echelon cubicles, closer to the windows and within earshot of Stu's office.

Quinn sniffed. "I know you two go back a long way, but watch your step. Jimmy knows Stu's thinking about making cuts. Stu asked me to rework the last story Jimmy submitted." Quinn pursed his lips and shrugged. "I'd hate to think you'd be caught in the middle."

"Middle?"

"That's right," Quinn said. "Between Jimmy and Stu."

Quinn pointed to his cubicle. "I've got a few leads to follow up on. Don't work too late." He smiled and walked away.

Violet shook her head, wondering what to make of the latest turn of events. After what had happened yesterday, Stu could easily decide she was the weak link in the editorial chain. Jimmy seemed to be standing on firmer ground.

Violet closed down her computer and grabbed her purse. She didn't want to think about decreased subscriptions and a declining economy and staff cuts that loomed on the horizon.

She needed the security of her home.

The thought of last night's intruder played through her mind.

Okay, her not-so-secure home. She'd follow Clay's advice and make some changes. Install a couple dead bolts, maybe an extra floodlight or two.

Glancing at the darkening sky outside, she tried to remember if she'd turned on a light this morning when she left for work.

Of course not.

Hopefully, Clay wouldn't be hanging around to rub her nose in her mistake.

A tingle of regret settled over her. Deep inside, she liked having the cop underfoot.

Stupid hormones, no doubt, which could get a girl in trouble. And that's exactly what Clay West was—trouble.

As night fell, Clay kept his eyes peeled on the Plaza Complex, waiting for Violet to leave the paper. He'd followed her back to work after their run-in at the coffee shop and parked on the street where he could see the front door of her building and the adjoining parking deck.

Grabbing his phone, Clay opened the photo file

to the picture he'd taken of the woman leaving the coffee shop. Violet wasn't the only one with a camera phone.

He sent the photo to Jackson's e-mail, then called the FBI agent. When he answered, Clay told him about Violet's aborted rendezvous with the woman on the run.

"I sent you her photo," Clay said. "See if you can identify the woman."

"Any idea who she is?"

"No clue. And she didn't hang around long enough for Violet to talk to her."

"We'll run the photo and let you know if we come up with anything."

"Thanks."

"Did Missoula P.D. find out anything about the punk you apprehended on Violet's street?"

"The guy played dumb for most of the morning. Officer O'Reilly said he broke shortly after noon."

"Hunger probably helped."

Clay chuckled. "No doubt. Jamie claims he was taking a circuitous route to meet up with a dealer who lives on the next block. Missoula P.D.'s had an influx of perpetrators come in from Spokane. They've known someone was selling in the neighborhood, but didn't have a name or location. They're staking out the druggie's house as we speak and hoping to make a bust as soon as they have probable cause."

"What about a possible connection with Chicago? Did they run a check on Jamie?"

"It's in the works. O'Reilly said he'd let me know if they uncover anything."

"Does the reporter realize she's had two close encounters?"

"You'd think she'd realize she might be in danger. Unfortunately, she was quizzing me over lunch about a possible next Mafia hit. She's convinced I'm in Missoula because the mob's coming after another green-eyed woman."

"Did you tell her if she continues to ask questions about the Martino family, she may be writing her own obit?"

Although Clay knew Jackson was trying to make a point, what he had said hit Clay hard. Cute and feisty though Violet was, her life was in danger. He needed to keep up surveillance so the mob wouldn't have an opportunity to take her out.

"From what we've gotten," Jackson continued, "the mob's focused on the Treasure State. There's talk of more women in danger. The U.S. Marshals are attempting to notify everyone in Witness Protection who fits the Mafia-hit profile."

Clay remembered what Violet had said. "Green eyes. Age twenty-one to forty. Attractive."

"That's right."

Violet fit the bill, except her eyes weren't green. They were brown. Big brown eyes that revealed so much of what she was trying to hold inside—her control, her desire to excel, her wit and charm.

"Listen, Clay, I've got another call. Let me know if anything new develops."

"Will do."

Clay disconnected and continued to watch the Plaza Complex, knowing Violet would eventually leave her office. He'd follow her home and keep her under surveillance tonight. She'd been in danger last night, and he may have thwarted two attempts to do her harm.

From what Jackson said, the mob was on the move to Missoula. Violet was too naive to see the danger, but Clay was well aware of what could happen if he let down his guard.

If he had to stick like glue to Violet to keep her safe, that's exactly what he'd do. Whether she liked it or not.

Approaching her house from the alleyway, Violet turned into the garage and hurried inside, locking the door behind her. Her answering machine blinked from her desk. She hit the play button and listened as a telemarketer started his spiel.

Delete.

The second call made her smile.

"Vi-o-let." Her neighbor Bernice used a long "o" for the middle vowel. "Come over when you get home from work. I've cooked a nice dinner and hope you can join me tonight."

Bernice's home cooking was hard to pass up. Plus, Violet had told Clay she had plans. Her neighbor's invitation proved she did. Violet was out the door before giving her decision a second thought.

The temperature had dropped with the setting sun. Luckily, Bernice didn't live far. The penetrating cold chilled Violet's bare hands. She rubbed them together as she climbed onto the porch and knocked on her neighbor's front door, glancing back at her own house to ensure she'd left the light on. The door creaked open behind her.

"If it isn't my old friend Violet Kramer."

She turned, realizing her self-control might be in danger again when she saw who was standing in the open doorway.

FIVE

"Your former commitment must have fallen through. I hope it wasn't anything important." Clay tried to keep from smirking. "There's a fire in the living room. Come in and get warm."

"Ah . . . what . . . are you . . . ?"

Violet acted as flustered as she had this afternoon at the newspaper. Her cheeks pinked from embarrassment. Both of them knew she hadn't been forthright about her plans for the evening. Of course, he hadn't mentioned his new lodging, either.

Bernice stepped from the kitchen. "Everything will be ready in a minute, Violet. Pot roast and mashed potatoes. Clay said you were friends in Chicago." The older woman smiled. "He saw my Room For Rent sign in the window and needed a place to stay. After that ruckus last night, I decided we could use a man around to keep us both safe."

"You've moved in with Bernice?" Violet glanced from Clay to Bernice and back to him again.

"The man's a gem." Bernice's face glowed with approval. "I told Clay about that leaky faucet in the back bathroom, and he's already fixed the problem."

Violet smiled, although the effort appeared painful. Clay imagined her mentally reviewing everything she'd said at the coffee shop and weighing whether dinner was worth having to put up with him. Hopefully, the mouthwatering aroma of Bernice's pot roast would convince her to stay.

"I was worried last night and asked the Lord to protect both of us," Bernice continued. "Then Clay appeared on my doorstep today. He's an answer to my prayer." She patted his arm and headed back to the kitchen.

The delightful landlady put more stock in his attempt to help than was deserved, but Bernice's stamp of approval must have had a positive effect because at that moment, Violet shrugged out of her coat and handed it to Clay.

"Did Bernice run an FBI check on you before you moved in?" she asked.

So that was the problem. "I'm just trying to keep you safe, Violet."

"And get me fired."

He hung her wrap in the hall closet then followed her into the living room. A couch, love seat and overstuffed chair sat around a brick fireplace where logs blazed.

"The fire's warm, and you look cold. Didn't your mother tell you to wear a hat and gloves in the winter?"

Violet threw him a frosty stare. "She was partial to mittens."

"Which you probably lost on occasion." He indicated for her to sit on the end of the couch closest to the fireplace. "I picture you as a free-spirit type of kid."

"More like strong willed. I don't give up." She raised her brows.

He got the message. She was determined to write the article on the mob and their connection to the two murdered Montana women.

"My mother called it my Aunt Lettie stubbornness," Violet added as she settled into the plush cushions on the couch.

"Her sister?"

"Sister-in-law." Violet's face shadowed for an instant.

"A favorite aunt?" he asked, hoping to determine the reason for the momentary change of expression.

"According to my mother, I followed in her footsteps." Violet failed to say more, and Clay wouldn't push the point.

She crossed her sculpted legs. He fought to keep his eyes from straying south, although he did glance at her shoes. Open toes and much too delicate for Missoula's winter. "You ever wear boots?"

She looked at her feet. "Only when it snows. Are you always so inquisitive? You sound more like a reporter than a cop."

"Look, Violet, we may have gotten off on the wrong foot last night and then again today."

She smiled. "You're going with a theme. Don't tell me you have a thing for feet?"

He swallowed down the laughter that tried to surface. The first comment that sprang to mind was he liked all parts of her anatomy, but that hardly seemed appropriate. Besides, their relationship needed to remain focused on the business at hand.

Her safety. What she knew about the Mafia. The name of her informant. All important topics that had nothing to do with shoes or feet or how he wanted to sit next to her on the couch.

Instead, he plopped down on the love seat. One guy in a two-person couch made him feel like the odd man out.

For the next few minutes, they chatted about Missoula and the scenic spots located in this section of the state, keeping the conversation neutral and safe.

Bernice stepped into the living room and invited them to the table. She led the way and explained the seating arrangement. "Clay, help Violet with the chair on my left. You sit to my right."

He held the indicated chair for Violet, then did the same for Bernice before he took his seat.

The savory smells made his mouth water. Bernice had cooked some of his favorites. Green beans, mashed potatoes and homemade rolls along with the roast and gravy.

Clay unfolded his napkin and laid it across his lap, waiting to dig in as soon as Bernice started to pass the various dishes.

Instead, she turned to him and gently touched his hand. "Such a pleasure having both of you at the dinner table this evening. We have so much for which to be thankful. I'd appreciate you offering the blessing, Clay."

"The blessing?"

"Why yes, Clay. We need to give thanks to God for the food." Bernice gave an inclusive glance at Violet. "And for the three of us being together."

At least, he had an idea of where to start. He *was* thankful to be with Violet. Surely he could put some of his feelings into words.

He bowed his head, dropped his hands to his lap and fiddled with his napkin under the table.

"Father . . . God, thank You for this food." He stole a glance at Violet. Her eyes were closed, hands clasped, head bowed. "And for allowing our paths to cross. We're grateful for Bernice's cooking and for our hungry appetites."

Bernice chuckled under her breath.

"Please keep Violet safe," Clay continued.

Her eyes popped open.

He winked. "Amen."

"That was lovely." Bernice's smile of gratitude was genuine. "The Lord gave you the right words this evening."

He looked across the table at Violet. Too bad he never seemed to have the right words to use with her. When he was around Violet, he felt as if he was out on a high ledge with nowhere to go but down.

She looked up again and her brown eyes locked on his.

The room shifted. She had a dangerous effect on his equilibrium as if he were standing on the edge of a mountain cliff and had just been struck with the random vertigo that sometimes flooded over him.

Step back or jump.

At this point, neither option made sense.

After dinner, Clay insisted on washing the dishes while Violet helped Bernice tidy the kitchen.

"Isn't he wonderful?" she whispered to Violet.

Seeing the muscular cop up to his elbows in soapsuds did soften the ambivalent feelings Violet had harbored toward Clay since he'd first appeared uninvited on her doorstep. She was beginning to realize the man had charm.

Once the dishes were dried and put away, Bernice fixed a pot of coffee then excused herself, claiming she needed her beauty sleep. Clay poured coffee, carried two mugs into the living room and sat next to Violet on the end of the couch closest to the fireplace.

"Heavy cream and two sugars. Did I get it right?"

"Perfect." She took a sip of the hot brew then leaned forward and placed her mug on the coffee table. Sitting back, she found Clay's arm curving around her shoulders.

He flashed her a hope-you-don't-mind smile that sent a jolt of electricity to her midsection. The scent of his aftershave brought back memories of a darkened alleyway in Chicago. Her head swam as if she were caught in a swift current, being carried downstream. For half a second, she thought he was going to kiss her.

Instead he said, "Why don't you tell me what you know. How'd you find out about the two murdered Montana women?"

Once a cop, always a cop.

Surely if she shared information, he would do the same. Plus, he might be able to open a door that had remained closed to her.

Violet told him how she learned about Ruby Summers Maxwell and the picture of Ruby's twin sister, Jade, standing with Marshal McGraw.

"His office handles Witness Protection," she explained. "Fairly obvious that Ruby was in the program."

"What about the other woman?"

"Carlie Donald entered Witness Protection after

testifying against a member of organized crime who worked in Philly."

"So the Martino family didn't have anything to do with her murder?" Clay asked.

"I never said that. Carlie wasn't killed because of the man she put in jail, but because of her green eyes and her participation in the Witness Protection Program."

"And green eyes are important because—?"

"Because Eloise Hill has green eyes. Years ago, when she testified against Salvatore Martino, her photo was in all the newspapers. I tracked down various stories in the archives. One of them mentioned her green eyes."

Violet had also learned Eloise had a child named Kristin, although she doubted the baby had any relevance to what happened in Montana. Violet decided to reveal what she'd learned about Clay.

"From what I found, your parents were killed in an auto accident. No relatives to take in their only child."

"No relatives *willing* to take in their only child," he corrected, frustration now evident in his voice.

"You were thirteen when you entered the Southside Foster Home and remained there for five years."

"I aged out at eighteen."

"Eloise was one of the other teens."

Clay nodded. "She was a few years older. For some reason, she decided to help the new kid settle in. Once I was Eloise's friend, the other kids accepted me."

"Testifying against Salvatore Martino forced her into Witness Protection."

"That's right." Clay nodded. "And her courage to go up against the Chicago don made me realize I wanted to work in law enforcement. Someone has to draw a line in the sand and say what's right and what's wrong or the bad guys win."

Violet shook her head ever so slightly. "You've known all along Eloise was the reason the Martino thugs killed the two women in Montana."

His lips twitched seductively. "Yeah, but I needed to find out how much you knew. You did your homework, Violet. Where'd you get the information?"

"A source who might be in danger."

"The woman at the coffee shop?" he asked.

Violet held up her hand. "I won't tell you anything until I talk to someone about getting her into the Witness Protection Program. I left a message with the U.S. Marshals office in Billings. Unfortunately, no one called me back."

"Earlier you mentioned Deputy Marshal Micah McGraw. I know his brother. Jackson McGraw is the FBI Special Agent-in-Charge of the Chicago office."

"Tell him I want protection for a woman associated with the mob."

Clay's brow furrowed. "I told you to be careful, Violet. We talked about how you are in danger. The Mafia doesn't play around."

"And what about other women who might be in danger? Shouldn't they be warned? At least they'd know the Mafia could be closing in if they read the article I'm writing, which exposes what's happening in this state."

"Printing something in the paper would blow the FBI operation and could endanger those already in Witness Protection."

"No, Clay, I'd be helping, not hurting their attempts to skirt the mob."

He sighed. "You're only seeing one side of the picture."

"And you're only interested in the side that affects you. What happened in Chicago that landed you in trouble? The way I heard it you pummeled a onetime pimp until backup arrived. You two had a history, only I couldn't find out what or who was involved."

Clay clamped down on his jaw.

She waited for him to respond. Maybe she'd gone too far.

He sat for a moment, staring at the fire. Finally, he grabbed their mugs off the coffee table and stood.

"It's late and you have to work tomorrow. I'll

get my coat." He took the mugs to the kitchen then walked to the back of the house. A door closed.

A few seconds later, Violet's phone rang. She pulled the cell from her purse and lifted it to her ear, hearing a sharp intake of breath before the connection died.

A Chicago area code but not the number Gwyn had used the night before last. Violet hit the call back button. Before anyone answered, Clay returned to the living room, coat in hand.

"I'll walk you home," he said.

Violet flipped her cell closed and stood. "Really, I'll be fine on my own."

He raised his brow.

She sighed. "Okay, I know. A girl's got to be careful."

He grabbed her coat from the closet and helped her slip it on. Shrugging into his own jacket, he held the door for her.

The night had turned even more frigid. Clay wrapped his arm around her shoulders as they hustled along the sidewalk. Violet's coat was lightweight, and she enjoyed the warmth of his embrace.

Stars twinkled overhead, and the moon—a bit larger than last night—lightened their path. As if there had been an unspoken pact, they turned to frivolous chatter that made them both laugh as they climbed the steps to Violet's porch. An inside lamp glowed through the window, and the porch light brightened the stoop.

Clay took the key from her hand and unlocked the door. "Let me check the house before you go in."

He quickly moved from room to room, opening closets and glancing behind furniture and into the corners. Tonight, Violet appreciated his concern for her safety.

He returned to the porch. "Everything looks okay. I noticed the laundry-room window was locked and the curtains drawn."

"I'm trying to do what you tell me," she said, feeling her lips twitch with mischief.

"Just remember the danger hasn't passed. I'll keep an eye on your house throughout the night so don't worry. My cell phone stays on. If you hear anything that doesn't sound right, call me."

"I don't need a bodyguard, Clay."

"Cut me a little slack, Violet."

He smiled in an alluring way that made her neck tingle and her internal temperature rise.

Quickly as it came, the smile vanished. Stepping closer, he caught her chin with his right hand and looked into her eyes.

Her heart skidded to a stop.

"Thanks for making my day a little brighter."

Violet sighed. The man had a way with words.

Then he turned on his heels and walked down the steps. Violet watched him hurry across the street, feeling a longing grow deep within her.

How could she sleep knowing he was on guard? The longer she was around Clay the more confused she became. As much as she wanted to stand on her own two feet, she let down her guard whenever he was near.

She needed to be careful. Yes, the mob posed a threat, but the way her body reacted whenever she was with Clay caused her more concern at the moment. Despite his good looks and rugged individualism, she needed to remember the bottom line.

She didn't trust cops.

SIX

Clay had acted like a love-struck teenager, wrapping his arm around his girlfriend as he walked her home. Fact was he'd wanted to kiss Violet. The thought tingled through his gut as he opened Bernice's front door and stepped inside the house. He would have liked to kiss Violet about a million times to see if that sensation ever subsided. Clay doubted it would.

Hanging his jacket in the closet, he noticed the fresh floral scent of Violet's perfume that clung to his shirt. He sniffed the sleeve that had wrapped around her on the couch then chuckled at his own reaction.

Get a grip, old boy.

Old? Thirty-five was hardly over the hill. But Violet had to be ten years younger. To him, the difference seemed insignificant. Age wasn't the problem.

He poured a cup of coffee, hoping the caffeine would snap him back to reality. He needed to talk to Jackson, but he didn't want the FBI agent to hear anything in his voice except a law officer's focus on his job.

Taking a long swig of the coffee, he pulled

out his cell and tapped in Jackson's number.

"I spoke with Violet Kramer," Clay said when the agent answered. "She's got friends who don't seem to have a problem feeding her information."

"Not surprising for a reporter."

"Violet mentioned an informant."

"The woman at the coffee shop?"

"I'm not sure, but the informant has some connection with the Martino family."

"Did you get a name?"

"No. Although we might be able to work out a deal if Violet can talk to someone in the U.S. Marshals office in Billings. She wants to get the informant into Witness Protection. I was hoping Micah would be available to meet with us."

"Any chance she'll share more information if we can promise protection for her snitch?"

"That's what I'm hoping. I'm also hoping she'll listen to Micah. My warnings haven't penetrated her stubbornness yet."

"I'll see what we can arrange," Jackson said.

"Violet mentioned Eloise."

"In what context?"

"Who the Mafia might be looking for."

"Did she get that from her source or come up with it on her own?"

"I have a feeling it was from the source. We know Salvatore wants Eloise to pay for sending him to jail."

Jackson grumbled. "What you did to Cameron

Trimble is what I'd like to do to Salvatore. Only I wouldn't want any cops around to pull me off the guy."

"I hear you."

"How many lives have been ruined because of him? How many people killed or living on the run?" Jackson pulled air into his lungs. "Listen, you're doing a good job with this reporter. I'll talk to Micah and get back to you."

Clay hung up and poured another cup of coffee. He'd keep watch over Violet's house to ensure the intruder or his buddies didn't return tonight. The way his heart was racing, Clay couldn't sleep. If he did nod off, he'd probably meet Violet in his dreams.

Still affected by her earlier encounter with Clay, Violet put water on the stove to boil, hoping a cup of chamomile tea would calm her fluttering heart. While the water heated, she opened her cell phone and looked at the last incoming number. Though the hang-up call had come from a Chicago area code, if it was from a cell phone, the caller could be anywhere. Even Missoula.

The kettle boiled. Violet poured water over the tea bag, inhaled the fresh herbal scent and, cup in hand, headed for her computer.

She had work to do. Somehow, she needed to shove Clay and the hang-up call into the think-about-later portion of her brain. Slipping her flash drive into the USB port, she pulled up the photo she'd taken on her cell phone earlier today.

The photo captured the woman's face as she'd glanced back at Violet. Or was she looking at something else?

Something or someone?

Minimizing the photo, Violet checked her e-mail and felt a surge of euphoria when a brief message from Gwyn flashed on the screen.

Are you online?

No reason to make small talk. Violet typed the question that had been bothering her all night.

Why'd you run away?

Someone was following you, came the reply.

Not the answer Violet had expected. She continued to read Gwyn's answer.

He looked familiar. Like a guy I'd seen in Chicago. Something about his build.

Could she have run into Clay when he was working undercover? Violet quickly typed:

Was it the undercover cop? The one who beat up Cameron Trimble?

Gwyn answered:

I don't know the cop. What's he look like?
The guy I saw was muscular. He wore a hat
so I'm not sure about his hair color.

Violet hit the reply button.

The undercover cop is—

What could she say about Clay? Tall, muscular
with eyes that sent shivers scurrying along her
spine?
Violet deleted the description and asked:

Are you sure someone was following me?

Gwyn: **Definitely.**
Violet: **Meet tomorrow?**
Gwyn: **Can't.**
Violet: **When?**
Gwyn didn't respond.
Violet's home phone rang. She glanced at the
clock. Almost midnight. The number failed to
appear on caller ID. Easy enough to block the
information. "Kramer."
Silence.
Violet glanced around her living room, glad
she'd pulled the drapes. "Hello?"
The sound of breathing caused the hair on the

back of her neck to rise. The caller inhaled. Exhaled. Slowly. Deliberately.

"Back off," a male voice whispered. The same message as on the note Clay had found.

Violet's stomach tightened. "Who is this?"

Another inhale.

She disconnected.

Violet picked up her cell and retried the number from the call she'd received at Bernice's house, as well as the number her informant had used night before last. Both failed to go through.

She needed to contact Gwyn, but the informant had refused to share her cell-phone number for fear Angelo would discover what was going on behind his back. In fact, Gwyn had made Violet promise never to reveal where she got her information to anyone.

Violet had kept that promise even when the *Gazette* editor had waved a permanent job in front of her face like a carrot. She'd lost the full-time position on the prestigious Chicago paper, but she'd been true to her word and never gave up her source.

Once again, the shrill ring of her landline echoed in the stillness of the house. Violet swallowed down the anxiety that swelled within her. Silly for a phone call to illicit such a response. Pulling in a determined breath, she reached for the receiver.

Inhale. Exhale.

"What do you want?" she demanded.

"Stay away from the mob."

Her cell rang. She glanced at the incoming number, noting a different Chicago area code, and flipped the phone open.

"Violet?" Clay's voice, concerned, urgent. "Your living room light is still on. Everything okay?"

"Someone called. He mentioned the mob."

"I'm coming over."

Before she could respond, her home phone rang again. She reached for the receiver and raised it to her ear. Silence. Then the rhythmic pull of air.

"Violet, let me in." Clay pounded on the front door.

He must have sprinted to get here so quickly. Relief swept over her as she threw open the door. Clay stood on the porch in his shirtsleeves, face flushed, windblown hair, looking like he'd kill anyone who hurt her.

Stepping inside, he grabbed the phone and spoke into the mouthpiece. "This is the police. I'm tracing your call, and I will find you."

He dropped the phone back to its cradle. "The creep hung up. What did he say to you?"

"To stay away from the mob."

Clay pursed his lips and nodded. "It's probably the same guy who broke into your home. Did you recognize anything about his voice?"

She tried to remember the cadence of his speech and any inflection that might have been familiar. Finally, she shook her head. "He spoke so quickly. Before I could process what he said, he'd hung up."

"I'll let Officer O'Reilly know what happened. Although I doubt he'd place a trace on your phone, unless the guy calls back again."

She shook her head. "I don't want the police coming over tonight. It's late." She pointed to her computer. "I've still got work to do."

"Then I'm staying," he insisted.

"Clay, please."

His gaze shifted to the front door. "You need dead bolts, Violet. There's an all-night discount store not far from here. I'll pick a couple up and install them tonight."

She held up her hand in protest. "Absolutely not. It's too late. I'll get the locks tomorrow. Maybe you could install them after work?"

"Yeah, sure. But I don't want you staying here alone. Grab your laptop and come over to Bernice's house. She's got a third bedroom that's not being used."

As inviting as the offer sounded, Violet needed to stay put. "I won't let a call frighten me out of my own home. The guy's a coward or he wouldn't have used the phone to warn me."

Clay's face twisted with disbelief. "He was standing in your kitchen last night, Violet."

"You can't be sure it was the same man."

Clay let out an exasperated sigh and raked his fingers through his short hair. "Is your Aunt Lettie as bullheaded as you?"

She bristled. "Was. Past tense. She died when I was a child."

His face softened. "I'm sorry about your aunt, Violet. But you need to accept the fact that the mob knows what you're doing. They've got someone watching you in Missoula. That person has warned you twice to back off. The next time might be more than a warning."

Of course, she knew he was right. She could no longer pretend the break-in and phone calls weren't connected, but she wouldn't—couldn't— stop her search for the truth. Women were being targeted. She needed to find out as much information as she could about the mob's activity in Montana. A news article exposing their murderous tactics would warn others who might be in danger.

"You'll be right across the street, Clay. I'll keep my cell on and call you if anything happens." She gave him a ragged smile. "Having a cop living in the neighborhood has its advantages."

The corners of his lips curled into a grin that rocked her to the core. Had to be 8.5 on the Richter scale. Why was he affecting her so much? Probably the late hour.

He stepped toward the door. "Call me if you need me."

"Thanks for your help."

"See you tomorrow night?"

"Yeah, sure." She locked the door behind him, feeling a letdown. As much as she'd wanted him to stay, the hour was late and she did have work to do. Clay would have been a distraction.

With a heavy sigh, Violet turned back to her computer and hit the refresh button. A new message appeared from Gwyn.

I planned to talk to you at the coffee shop about another woman in Witness Protection. Angelo got information before I left Chicago. I've attached the photo he received. Her name's Jen Davis. The mob's after her. She's next on their list. Mama's Diner in Billings plays into it somehow.

Violet opened the attachment and stared at the photo. The woman was pretty with a sweet smile and long brown hair pulled into a ponytail. She wore what appeared to be a white nurse's uniform and stared back at Violet with green expressive eyes. Printing off a color copy, Violet shook her head as the ink dried.

She scribbled Ruby and Carlie's names on a piece of scrap paper. Underneath, she wrote Jen Davis followed by a question mark. Jen Davis was in the crosshairs of the mob. She needed to be warned.

Violet searched the white pages online. No Jen, Jenny or Jennifer Davis was listed in Billings, which meant she probably used a cell phone.

Plugging Mama's Diner into a map search, Violet found a hospital, nursing home and six doctors' offices located within a few blocks of the restaurant.

Although the hour was late, she requested the diner's phone number from directory assistance. Tapping the digits into her cell, she heard a recorded message. "Mama's Diner is closed for the night. Call back when we're open for business—7:00 a.m. to 9:00 p.m."

The mobsters had mentioned Mama's Diner, so the place had to have significance. Maybe Jen worked there. Maybe she was a frequent customer. Surely someone would know her or recognize her name.

Unless she used an alias.

A woman's life was in danger, and Violet was stuck in Missoula. On a whim, she checked the airlines. The distance from Missoula to Billings was over 350 miles. Too far to drive there and back in one day, but a flight left at 8:00 a.m. and returned at 4:00 p.m.

Before she had time to change her mind, Violet purchased a round-trip ticket to Billings then printed off the boarding pass and electronic ticket. She sent an e-mail to Stu saying she planned to work from home tomorrow, which he'd get when he arrived at the paper in the morning.

A noise outside pulled her attention from the laptop. Her heart thumped a warning. She reached for her cell, ready to call Clay when a knock sounded at her front door.

"Honey, it's Bernice."

Violet opened the door, surprised to find her neighbor wrapped in a thick flannel robe, hair disheveled and clutching her pillow.

The older woman threw her thumb over her shoulder. "I got up for a drink of water and found Clay hunkered down on the front porch. The man insists he needs to keep watch over your house. I told him it made more sense if we both spent the night at your place."

Violet looked around her neighbor to where Clay stood on the sidewalk. He smiled like a little boy who'd been caught with his hand in the cookie jar.

Bernice stepped past Violet and headed for the back hallway. "I've got the guest room. Clay said he'd sleep on the couch. See you two in the morning."

Clay stretched out his hands and shrugged as he climbed the steps to the porch. "I told Bernice I was fine, but she wouldn't take no for an answer. Any chance she's related to your Aunt Lettie?"

Violet had to smile. "No, but she's equally determined. Come in where it's warm. Surely you didn't plan to keep watch all night?"

He followed her into the living room. "Of course not."

His reply sounded anything but truthful. Clay was skewing her usually low opinion of law enforcement. The guy wouldn't let up where her safety was concerned. Not that she was complaining. In fact, Violet was starting to enjoy having him around.

"Would you like a cup of coffee?" she asked.

"No, thanks." He glanced at her laptop. "I know you've got work to do. I'll just stretch out on the couch."

Violet grabbed a blanket, sheets, pillow and pillowcase from the laundry room and returned to find him staring at the photo of Jen Davis and the note with her name scribbled under Ruby Maxwell and Carlie Donald.

"Your informant contacted you again?" he asked.

No reason to keep the information from him. Violet shared what Gwyn had told her. "The mob thinks Jen's in Billings. I'm flying there tomorrow."

His eyes widened. "You're what?"

She held up her hands. "Just for the day. I want to go to Mama's Diner and see if anyone recognizes her from the photo. Jen needs to know she's in danger."

"Which you are, as well, Violet."

"You can't talk me out of going, Clay."

"Then I'll get a ticket and fly there with you."

A warmth spread over her. "You'd do that for me?"

"It's my job to keep you safe."

Job? Was that why he'd been so attentive?

Violet pulled the flash drive from the USB port but left her computer running. "You can use my laptop to make your flight reservation. Help yourself to anything that's in the fridge."

Clay's brow furrowed. "Did I say something wrong?"

She shook her head. "No, of course not, but it's been a long day, and I'm tired. Check the doors before you go to sleep, and I'll see you in the morning."

She hurried back to her bedroom and closed the door behind her, relieved to have some privacy. Clay filled her living room with too much of a male presence.

Silly of her to think his concern for her went beyond his duty. Cops were trained to defend and protect. That's what Clay was doing. No more. No less.

Violet tried to sleep, but she kept thinking about who was stretched out on her living-room couch.

The light from the hallway shone under the door. Evidently, she hadn't turned it off. No doubt, it would bother Clay's sleep, as well.

Throwing on her robe, Violet tiptoed into the hallway and glanced into the living room. Clay was sound asleep. The top of the blanket had fallen to the floor. Violet stepped closer and placed it over his shoulders.

Glancing at her desk, she spied his electronic airline ticket next to her own. The screen saver flickered across the screen. Might as well turn everything off.

She tapped a key and the home page for the Billings newspaper returned to the screen. Had Clay uncovered more information on Jen Davis?

Violet hit the BACK icon and watched as a photograph and story unfolded. She scanned the text.

Billings lawyer Barton Perry—known for civic outreach—and his wife, Anna, killed in a tragic automobile accident . . . survived by only-child, Kristin, currently attending the University of Westbrook . . . the Perrys had worshipped at Faith Church in Billings.

Violet enlarged the photo. Mr. and Mrs. Barton stood next to their daughter.

Kristin? The same name Eloise had given her baby girl who had been adopted years ago. Violet did the math. Kristin would have been college age by now.

Violet leaned closer to the monitor and compared the young woman's likeness to the news photos of Eloise she'd uncovered in the *Chicago Gazette* archives. The resemblance was striking.

She glanced at Clay, sleeping peacefully. Had he been interested in the photo and article because of his old friend from Southside Foster? The mob wanted to find Eloise. Hopefully, they wouldn't try to find her daughter, as well.

Violet closed out of the newspaper's site then turned off the computer and retraced her steps back to her bedroom, switching the hall light off as she went.

She'd let Clay keep his secret about Kristin. The less anyone knew about the young woman the better.

Keep her safe, Lord. Keep all the women safe.

SEVEN

As the sun rose on the horizon, Clay left Bernice and Violet sleeping while he walked across the street to Bernice's house. He showered, changed into a starched shirt and khakis and fixed a pot of coffee. Strong and black.

Glancing into the living room, his eyes rested on the couch where Violet had sat last night.

He couldn't stop thinking about her sparkling eyes and inviting smile and the way her hair had felt like silk against his arm. The desire to draw her into his embrace had stayed with him through the night.

The house was chilly. Knowing Bernice would return home soon, Clay arranged crumpled newspaper around a bundle of kindling in the fireplace. Striking a match, he held it to the wood.

The flame spread as fast as corruption did in Chicago. Clay shook his head, thinking back to what had happened. He had worked so hard trying to learn the name of the person who ran the prostitution racket for the mob. One name. That's what he'd been after for too long.

The way the mob exploited women sickened him, and going undercover meant mingling with men who cared nothing about the people they hurt.

The smell of burning wood swirled around him, warming the room, but his thoughts turned to the cold night when all his hard work and the efforts of the law-enforcement team that had set up the sting should have paid off.

Everything went wrong when Cameron Trimble stepped on to the scene. He had recognized Clay. Working undercover was dangerous. Being exposed could cost a man his life.

Using the end iron, Clay adjusted the logs. The fire sputtered and crackled. A log shifted, sending sparks into the air.

Clay had fought for his life that night. Luckily, backup had arrived in time.

Flames licked at the logs. Clay stared into the fire. The Bible said Christ was the light of the world. He remembered that much from what Eloise had told him. She said God could transform evil and allow good to come from the bad.

Could something good come from his run-in with Cameron Trimble? If Clay hadn't been on probation, he wouldn't have been free to help Jackson. Since Clay had come to Montana, he'd felt an inner sense of completeness as if part of him that had been unraveled was starting to knit together. For the first time in a long while, he had hope that the future could be filled with something good.

Was Violet the reason?

Or was he fooling himself?

"Morning, Clay." Bernice let herself in and headed for the kitchen. He retraced his steps and found her pouring a cup of coffee, her flannel bathrobe wrapped around her waist. "Sure is nice to have the coffee ready. Thanks."

She smiled at him, like the grandmother he'd never known. "You're worried about Violet, aren't you?"

"She's too independent for her own good."

Bernice nodded. "You're right. I've been praying someone special would come into her life."

Warmth spread over Clay that had nothing to do with the crackling fire or the hot coffee.

"I told God she needed a good man." Bernice's eyes crinkled. "Looks like the Lord sent you."

Clay didn't know if that was a compliment or a challenge. No matter how assured he tried to be on the outside, inside he knew the truth. He didn't deserve Violet. After everything that had happened in his life, he didn't deserve anyone.

As Bernice prepared her breakfast, Clay grabbed his jacket from the closet and, after saying goodbye, headed for his car. Violet ran out from her house when he pulled to the curb.

"Did you lock your doors?" he asked as she slipped into the passenger seat.

"Of course. Plus, I rechecked the windows and left the drapes drawn."

Maybe Violet had finally realized she needed to be careful.

But what about him? He needed to be careful, as well. He stole a glance at her. She seemed oblivious to his perusal. The winter sun bathed her in light that made her eyes sparkle and her lips shine.

Keeping Violet safe from the mob was his number-one problem. His growing attraction for her was a close second.

Violet and Clay grabbed coffee and bagels at an airport kiosk, and ate breakfast before boarding.

Mechanical problems delayed takeoff, and once airborne, the flight was bumpy due to turbulence. Luckily, the landing was smooth and, after disembarking, they followed the signs to car rental and were soon heading to Mama's Diner.

Road construction slowed their progress, but they eventually found a parking spot in front of the diner and hurried inside. The early lunch crowd was already filling the small establishment.

Violet stood next to Clay as they waited for a table and scanned the folks already seated.

"Do you see anyone resembling the woman in the photo?"

"No, but I don't like the clientele," he said.

She followed his gaze to a guy sitting in the corner, wearing a hooded sweatshirt. Violet hadn't noticed him earlier.

"Check out the last booth on the right," Clay said under his breath.

She turned ever so slightly. Another man. This one wore a couple-days growth of beard and a black beanie pulled low over his forehead.

Standing close to Clay, she had no sense of fear, yet she was beginning to understand how a cop's mind worked. Clay was always looking for trouble, second-guessing who might be involved with the mob. Maybe she needed to readjust her attitude and be a bit more cautious, although with Clay to protect her, she hardly needed to worry.

A friendly waitress showed them to a booth by the window. "The lunch special's meatloaf and mashed potatoes. Green beans or corn on the side."

Violet opted for a house salad and a cup of vegetable soup. Clay ordered a burger and fries. A layer of clouds hung low over the city. A storm was forecast to roll into Missoula in the next couple of days. All signs pointed to Billings being hit sooner.

When the waitress left to get coffee for both of them, Violet leaned toward Clay. "How do you want to handle this? Good cop, bad cop?"

He smiled. "How 'bout, good cop and reporter? Remember, we're a team."

"Got it."

The waitress quickly returned with two mugs of steaming coffee.

"We're looking for a woman who may work around here." Violet held up the photo she'd printed off her computer.

"Her name's Jen Davis. Do you know her or recognize her picture?"

"No, but I'll ask the other gals. Maybe one of them can help you." She took the photo and showed it to the other waitresses working the floor.

A short time later, she returned to the table with their lunch order and the photo. "No one knows your friend. From the white uniform she's wearing, I take it she's a nurse. There's a hospital close by. Have you thought about stopping there?"

"That's where we plan to go next," Violet said.

"We change shifts at two. You might want to come back and talk to the waitresses on duty then."

As much as she wanted to find Jen Davis, Violet was starting to realize the trip to Billings might not prove successful after all, and that worried her.

Clay remained in cop mode, flicking his gaze from the man in the hoodie to the guy wearing the beanie. Once both men had finished eating, paid their checks and left the diner, Clay relaxed.

The cop took his job seriously and Violet appreciated his support. Working as a team wasn't so bad after all. Then she thought of the story she needed to publish that would expose the mob's move into Montana.

Ruby Maxwell, Carlie Donald and now Jen Davis.

No matter what Clay said, women in Witness Protection needed to be warned.

When the waitress brought the check, Violet excused herself to use the ladies' room. On the way back to the table, she stopped to study a bulletin board decorated with photos taken inside the diner. Many of the waitresses working today were featured in the collage.

One woman's profile caught Violet's eye. She leaned closer to examine the picture.

Violet had kept in touch with a few reporters on the *Chicago Gazette.* One of them had sent her a photograph of Olivia Jensen, the woman who had witnessed Vincent Martino kill a man in cold blood. Olivia was being held in protective custody until the trial this spring.

Last night, Violet had mentally compared the photo of Kristin Perry with Clay's friend, Eloise. The two women had a similar appearance as if related, but the woman in the bulletin-board photo today looked identical to the photo of Olivia.

Violet called over one of the waitresses she'd talked to earlier. "Do you know how I could get in touch with the woman in this photo?"

"Olivia Jarrod?" The waitress shook her head.

"I heard she left town. The manager tried to find her, but couldn't."

Olivia Jarrod had to be Olivia Jensen, the woman whose testimony could send Vincent Martino to jail. No wonder the mob was interested in the diner. Maybe the trip hadn't been a waste of time after all.

Violet headed back to Clay. He stood as she neared the table. Better to keep the information about Olivia to herself. As much as she liked Clay, he was law enforcement.

Bottom line, she didn't trust cops.

Clay took Violet's hand as they left the diner and headed for the rental car. They spent the next few hours checking the hospital, nursing homes and doctors' offices in the area. No one named Jen Davis or who looked like her picture was employed at any of the health-care facilities.

Tired and frustrated, they returned to the diner shortly after two. The crowd had dwindled, and only a handful of customers sat at tables. They ordered coffee to go and asked the same questions they had earlier with the same results.

This time when they left the diner, Violet was visibly discouraged. As Clay opened the passenger door for her, he caught sight of a man standing across the street, wearing a dark sweatshirt with the hood pulled up. Was he the same guy they'd seen eating earlier?

"Sir?" Someone called. He turned. One of the waitresses hurried toward them.

"I've been thinking about that picture you showed me," she said, nearing the car. "There's a woman who stops in for lunch occasionally. Her hairstyle's different, but she could be the gal you need to find. She was friends with one of the waitresses, only she hasn't been at work for a few days. Someone said they think Olivia left town."

Clay pursed his lips. "Olivia?" Not the most common of names.

"Yeah, Olivia Jarrod. But she's moved on. A couple weeks ago, I saw the woman you're looking for walking along the main road and offered her a lift."

"Do you remember where you dropped her?" Violet asked.

"An apartment not far from here." The waitress provided the address. Clay thanked her. When he looked back across the street, the man in the hooded sweatshirt had disappeared. Clay pulled in a deep breath. Could the guy who broke into Violet's home have followed them to Billings? Or was Clay becoming too paranoid?

He needed to follow his gut, which was telling him to be on guard. The mob didn't play by any rules. They'd kill an innocent woman without blinking an eye.

He slipped behind the wheel and drove to the address the waitress had provided.

"I hope she's here," Violet said as they walked into the building and knocked on a door marked Manager.

An older woman, gray hair in a bun, stuck her head out. "You looking for a furnished place to rent?"

"No, ma'am." Violet held out Jen's photo. "We're looking for this woman. Someone told us she lived here."

"That's right." The manager nodded. "Hannah Williams lived here, but she moved out a few days ago. She paid her rent with cash and didn't leave a forwarding address."

"Did Hannah have any friends or other neighbors who might know how to find her?" Clay asked.

"She stayed to herself. I never saw anyone visit."

Clay shared Violet's frustration as they climbed back into the car.

His neck tingled. He glanced in the rearview mirror. Nothing.

Turning, he studied the apartments across the street. A man peered at them from around the far corner of the building.

He wore a dark sweatshirt and a beanie.

"Stay here, Violet. Lock the doors."

Clay raced across the street in pursuit of the guy who took off running.

Rounding the rear of the building, Clay stopped short. He'd lost the guy again.

Letting out a frustrated groan, Clay backtracked. As he approached the car, his gut tightened.

Violet's hand clutched her neck, her eyes wide, face blanched.

"What happened?" he demanded as he opened the door.

She stumbled into his arms. "A . . . a car rounded the corner and headed right for me. I—" She tried to catch her breath. "I thought he was going to hit your car. He swerved in the nick of time."

"Did you see the driver?"

She shook her head. "It happened too fast."

Clay wrapped Violet in his arms feeling her heart pound in her chest. He glanced at the apartments on both sides of the road. The curtains were drawn. No one appeared to have seen the incident.

"Come on, honey, we're going to the Marshals office. We'll talk to Micah McGraw. He needs to know what happened."

She shook her head, gathering control. "Probably just some kids driving too fast."

Clay held the door as she climbed into the passenger seat. One thing bothered him about Violet. She had closed her mind to the real danger that surrounded her. Clay hadn't been imagining the men in the restaurant or on the street. Violet's informant knew about Mama's Diner, and she got her information from the mob. Their men were lying in wait for Jen Davis. Now they knew the inquisitive reporter from Missoula was interested in her whereabouts, as well. As worried as he'd been in Missoula, Clay was even more worried about Violet's safety in Billings.

When they arrived at the Marshals headquarters, they learned Micah was out of town on business. Mac Sellers, an older guy who walked with a limp, assured Clay he'd be happy to pass on any information they had to Micah.

"That won't be necessary," Violet said to Sellers as she nudged Clay toward the door. "We'll contact Agent McGraw later in the week. Thanks for your help."

Once outside, Clay turned to her. "Why didn't you want to talk to the agent on duty?"

"You don't know him, Clay. Neither do I. Call it woman's intuition, but I didn't want to share information about Jen with a stranger."

Violet's concern for the woman's safety touched Clay's heart. She had spunk and determination, which he admired. Clay felt sure Jackson could arrange a meeting with Micah someplace other than in Billings. He never wanted Violet back in this town again. At least not until the Martino family was in jail.

Clay had seen Faith Church earlier on their way to the diner. Now he pulled to the curb in front of the office attached to the sacristy.

"Come inside with me, Violet. I need to talk to someone."

Surprised when she didn't ask any questions, he escorted her into a lobby.

"I'll wait for you here," she said, settling into a chair outside the main office. She reached for a Bible on the side table and opened the scriptures.

He spoke to the receptionist who escorted him into the pastor's office.

Reverend Taylor was a big man with a warm smile. Clay quickly explained he was concerned about Kristin Perry's safety. The pastor admitted he'd been praying for her since learning about her parents' tragic deaths, but he hadn't seen her.

"She's searching for her birth mother," Clay explained. "A woman I knew years ago. Without going into information that needs to be kept confidential, I'm worried Kristin might be in danger if she continues making inquiries about her mother. If she does contact you, would you encourage her to rely on law enforcement? The U.S. Marshals office here in Billings could help her or she could contact me." Clay gave his card to the reverend. "She can call me on my cell anytime."

"Sounds like you're a caring man, Clay. If Kristin contacts me, I'll do as you asked. Until then, I'll continue to pray for her and for you. May the Lord bless you and keep you safe."

Clay left the office, feeling a new sense of peace. Violet smiled as he approached her.

"Ready?"

She nodded and stood. Taking his outstretched hand, she said, "Eloise must have been a special woman, and you're a great guy to be concerned about the daughter."

Violet seemed to be able to read his mind. As intuitive as she was, he wished she were more aware of his concern for her safety.

He felt a sense of relief when they boarded the plane.

Violet fell asleep shortly after takeoff, resting her head on his shoulder. Careful not to wake her, he wrapped his arms around her shoulders and drew her close.

Clay couldn't take his eyes off her throughout the flight. Teaming up with Violet had been a good decision. She was starting to trust him, and he felt the same about her. In fact, he was feeling a lot of things right now, especially a desire to stay in Missoula and get to know the sleepyhead reporter even better.

Her eyes blinked open when the plane touched down.

"Morning," he whispered.

"Oh, I'm sorry. I must have dozed off."

"Not a problem." Truth was he'd liked holding her in his arms. She straightened, and he instantly regretted the flight had come to an end.

Clay drove her home and pulled to a stop in front of her house. He glanced at Bernice's home. She'd left the front-porch light on for him.

"Looks like she's asleep," Violet said, following his gaze. "I'll be fine tonight. Let Bernice sleep, and you do the same."

"Bernice did look tired this morning. But you have to promise to call if you suspect anything is amiss."

"Promise."

He crawled out of the car and rounded the front to open the passenger door. He'd let Violet think she was on her own, but he'd remain vigilant throughout the night. He wouldn't give the mob an opportunity to strike.

Taking her hand, they walked to the porch.

"Thanks for letting me help today," he said once they were at her door. "In my opinion, we make a good team."

Violet nodded, her eyes on his. "It was nice working together for a change," she admitted.

"Trust me, okay? We're on the same page."

Clay took her keys, opened her door and quickly searched inside.

"Call me if you need anything," he said after returning to the porch. They were standing close and neither made an effort to step apart.

Violet stared up at him with her twinkling eyes, a bit puffy from her nap on board the plane. Her lips parted as if she were going to say something.

Clay's heart pounded in his chest. Violet looked so soft and inviting that he couldn't help himself. He touched her cheek and lowered his mouth to hers. Her lips were warm and sweet.

When he finally pulled back, she sighed and, without saying a word, stepped inside, closing the door behind her.

Clay stood on the porch long enough for the world to stop spinning. Then he crossed the street and walked to Bernice's house.

Kissing Violet was the best thing he'd done in a very long time. In fact, he wanted to make a habit of kissing her on a regular basis. But when he thought of the limited time he'd be staying in Missoula, his mood sobered. As much as he liked being with Violet, she wasn't interested in him other than for the help he could provide.

Clay was a cop first. He needed to act like one.

EIGHT

Violet had trouble keeping her mind on her work the next day. She kept thinking about Clay's kiss. Stu had assigned her a number of fillers to write that required tracking down bits of information and kept her occupied throughout the morning. The editorial update meeting after lunch had gone longer than normal, and she was eager to get back to her computer and check her Web site and e-mail.

Hurrying back to her desk, Violet took a short-cut by the elevators. Rounding the partition, she found Clay sitting in her swivel chair, fiddling with the computer she'd turned off before she went to the update.

Her heart did a double take when he looked up and grinned. "I wondered when you'd get back to work."

She ignored the way her lips tingled where he'd kissed her and tried to act nonchalant as she glanced at the monitor. "Sudoku?"

"Addicting, isn't it?"

She reached around his broad shoulders and closed the page. "How'd you get my password?"

His face only inches from her own, she smelled

his aftershave, a woodsy scent that made her knees weak. Needing support, she braced against the edge of her desk, noting the tiny scar on his chin and the dimple in his right cheek when he grinned, which was what he was doing right now.

Grinning and moving closer. *Déjà vu* of last night. His aftershave alone was enough to crash her mainframe. And she wasn't talking about her computer.

"You haven't answered me." She pulled back, giving herself space and air. She couldn't think straight when he was close to her. "How'd you log on?"

"Your computer was up and running, Violet."

"No, it wasn't."

He winked. "Cross my heart."

Another surge to her power source.

Maybe she hadn't closed out of everything. She tried to remember. Why was she getting so confused recently? Had to be that aftershave and the memory of his kiss.

Clay glanced at his watch. "Micah McGraw's in town. He agreed to see us."

The password issue no longer seemed important. Violet turned off her computer, grabbed her coat and purse and raced after Clay, who held the elevator door open.

"We're meeting him at Police Headquarters," Clay said. "Micah should be there by the time we arrive."

Police? As in Chief Howard? Not her favorite person, but she wouldn't turn down the opportunity to talk to Marshal McGraw. As long as she stayed far enough from Clay so her mind could function, she'd be all right. Get too close to him, and all her good intentions would be for naught.

Clay escorted Violet into the conference room where Micah McGraw stood waiting. Tall, lean and wiry, he was a casual reflection of his brother dressed in a blue shirt and jeans.

The Marshal's brown eyes were warm as he stepped around the long rectangular table and greeted them with a firm handshake. Clay eyed the Stetson on a nearby table and a heavy parka thrown over the back of a chair.

"Pleasure to meet you," he said returning Micah's handshake. The Marshal indicated a chair for Violet on his left. Clay sat across the table from her. She appeared calm and in control, exactly as Clay had expected her to act.

"Let's start at the beginning. Jackson said you have information about the two women murdered in Montana?" Micah seemed as straightforward as his brother. Younger, but equally as focused.

Violet repeated what she'd told Clay.

"So you deduced the women were in Witness Protection when you saw a picture of Jade with me?"

"That's right. I found your name in a listing of U.S. Marshals."

A muscle in Micah's neck twitched.

"Your office handles Witness Protection," Violet continued. "I made the connection."

"And did you receive information from a Mafia informant?"

"Yes, a contact in Chicago. Her boyfriend works for the Martino family and that's how she gets her information. My informant believes both women were targeted by the crime family."

"What else did your source say?"

"She sent an e-mail that mentioned Eloise Hill."

The same muscle in Micah's neck twitched as he flicked his gaze to Clay.

Oblivious to the look that passed between the two men, Violet explained what she knew about the woman who had testified against the old don, Salvatore Martino. Violet concluded by saying, "The Martino family somehow has figured out that Eloise was placed in the Witness Protection Program in Montana, and they've been hunting down and killing women in the program in this state, hoping one of them will be Eloise."

"Is that your take or the source's?" Micah asked.

"My source verbalized it first. But it's obvious, isn't it?"

"Do you have any additional information about your Chicago informant?"

"We communicate online. She's called me a few times but always using a disposable phone. If I try to call her back, a recording says the number's no longer in operation."

Violet hesitated a moment before continuing. "We were going to meet at a coffee shop near the UMT campus, but she thought someone was following me and fled. Someone she recognized from Chicago."

The Marshal glanced at Clay. "It wasn't me. I was tailing Violet, but the gal in the coffee shop never saw me."

"Someone scared her off," Violet insisted. "She's on the run and needs protection."

"Did your source ask for your help?" Micah asked.

The look on Violet's face didn't require explanation. She had cooked up the plan on her own to get the woman into Witness Protection. True to character, Violet was sticking her nose where it didn't belong. As much as Clay applauded her desire to help, she was putting herself in danger at the same time.

Micah explained his hands were tied unless the informant was willing to turn herself over to the authorities. No matter what Violet wanted, the mob girlfriend might not want protection, which was what Clay was beginning to think about Violet. She kept ignoring his warnings to be careful.

The Marshal straightened in his chair, apparently ready to end the meeting. "As I mentioned, Violet, I can't move forward on this unless you can assure me the source is interested in working with my office and willing to provide evidence against the Mafia."

Violet offered a weak smile. "There's something else." She pulled the picture of Jen Davis from her purse and handed it to Micah. "The informant said the mob's looking for this woman. She's in Witness Protection. Her name's Jen Davis. My informant heard her boyfriend mention Mama's Diner in Billings."

Clay explained about the apartment where Jen had lived until a few days ago. He wrote down the address and handed the paper to Micah.

"We've been concerned about Jen. The FBI is tracking down all young women with green eyes in Witness Protection." There was a sense of urgency in Micah's voice that hadn't been evident earlier. "We'll focus on the address you provided and see what we can uncover."

Micah concluded the meeting with a dose of advice for Violet about staying clear of the mob and not bringing trouble upon herself.

She'd heard the same message more than once from Clay but hadn't taken what he had said to heart. If only she'd be swayed by Micah.

The Marshal repeated his offer to help Violet's informant should she be interested, then he stood and shook their hands. Clay expressed his gratitude for seeing them so quickly.

"I had to be in town on business," Micah said. "I'm glad it worked out." The genuineness in his smile and the concern in his eyes reminded Clay of Jackson.

"Let me know if you learn anything new about Jen Davis," Clay said. "Once the informant comes forward, she may have more information."

"We'll pass everything on to you, Clay. I promise."

Clay placed his arm on the small of Violet's back as they left the office. He guided her through a maze of corridors, heading to the side door and the parking lot. As they rounded the last corner, a man in uniform—early fifties, silver-tipped hair —walked toward them. Even without reading his name tag, the rank on his uniform left no doubt he was Chief of Police Walter Howard.

"Sir." Clay extended his hand and introduced himself.

The chief nodded. "Jackson McGraw mentioned you were in town. Stop by my office so we can talk sometime." He turned to Violet. "I haven't seen your parents in a while, Violet. I hope they're doing well."

"They're fine, thank you." Without further comment, she stepped around the chief and continued down the hallway.

"Have a good day, sir," Clay mumbled, hastening to catch up with her.

Memo to self—find out what the friction was between Violet and the chief. Clay held the door for her. She hurried into the cold, no hat or mittens, coat open wide.

What was she thinking about? Micah? The women she wanted to save? Or her ill feelings toward the chief of police?

NINE

Deep in thought, Violet had little to say on the way back to her office. Clay seemed to understand. She had hoped Micah would help her free Gwyn from the control of the mob, but he needed more information and an assurance she would provide evidence and testify against the Mafia.

Gwyn had undermined the mob's control every time she slipped information to Violet, and she'd finally escaped her boyfriend's control. But as scared as she had looked fleeing from the coffee shop, Violet doubted Gwyn would agree to working with the law.

For Violet, coming face-to-face with the chief of police had brought back vivid memories of everything that had happened so long ago in her hometown of Granite Pass. A number of the officers on the force had shoved her dad around, but she never recalled Wayne Howard being involved. Had she misjudged him over the years?

Violet had gone into journalism to right a wrong that had happened when she was only seven years old. Her mantra—the core principle that shaped her work in journalism—was *Protect the Innocent,* especially those wrongly accused. The finger of guilt, even when misdirected, had a long memory.

As much as she hated to open old wounds, maybe she needed to have a heart-to-heart with her dad about the facts as she remembered them. He and her mom had reestablished themselves in the community and had moved on from that terrible time in their lives. Violet seemed to be the only one who still struggled with the past.

When Clay pulled to the curb in front of the Plaza Complex, Violet hesitated before opening the door. "Are you going back to Bernice's house now?"

"Actually, I planned to hang around downtown until you get off work." He winked. "Just in case you need me."

Heat tingled her spine. His looks did the oddest things to her insides. Right now they felt like mush. "I won't be too much longer. There's a coffee shop on the first floor and an alcove with chairs on the third floor just to the right of the elevators. That is, if you need a place to hang out."

"Are you worried about your safety?"

"No, of course not. I just don't want you arrested for loitering. Missoula isn't Chicago, you know." Her lips twitched. "Guys don't wait around on street corners, waiting to pick up girls around here."

He laughed out loud, a good sound that turned her internal thermostat up a notch.

"Let me find a parking place, then I'll come inside. Can I buy you a coffee?"

"No, thanks. See you in a few minutes." Violet hurried inside and rode the elevator to the third floor. Settling into the swivel chair behind her desk, she booted up her computer.

Jimmy neared and handed her a stack of photos. "Take a look at these and tell me what you think."

Violet admired the quality of his work. He was talented, and his college hobby was beginning to have a professional quality. "You should talk to Stu about spending more time with the photographers on staff."

"Trying to get rid of me, eh?" He was smiling, but she saw something in his eyes that was far from humorous.

Quinn's words came to mind about watching her back, especially around Jimmy.

Violet wanted to check her e-mail to see if Gwyn had left a message, but knowing Jimmy's wandering eye, she clicked on her document files instead and waited for the listing to appear on the screen.

While he continued to study his own photos, Violet scrolled through her folders, searching for the information she'd compiled on police recruitment. She found the documents she needed but noticed the folder on the Martino crime family wasn't in its rightful place.

"Violet, what's he doing here?" Jimmy asked, peering over the partition.

She peeked around the divider and saw Clay sitting in the alcove near the elevators. Arms crossed over his chest, he smiled back at her, looking totally at ease.

"Excuse me." She left Jimmy at her desk and scurried into the hallway. Clay stood as she neared.

"Do you want today's newspaper to read or a magazine?" she asked.

"I thought I'd pass the time by watching you work." His eyes twinkled, and his lips curled into a grin that made her knees weak.

She glanced into the newsroom at the reporters bent over their computers. None of them seemed to notice the man who had taken up residence in the alcove. Except Jimmy, who glared at both of them.

The grin left Clay's face. "Is that kid giving you a hard time?"

"Jimmy?" She shook her head. "He just likes to complain."

"Well, let me know if he complains too much. Now get back to work and stop worrying about me."

"Yes, sir." She turned on her heel and clipped back to her desk where Jimmy waited.

"You need to be careful, Violet."

Advice everyone seemed to be giving her recently. She refocused on her computer files and did a search for the Mafia folder she'd compiled.

Jimmy rounded her desk and leaned over her shoulder. "Problem?"

"I can't find some of my files."

"Check your recycle bin. Maybe you inadvertently deleted them."

She followed his suggestion and found a few discarded files but none involving Chicago crime.

Jimmy flipped his thumb toward the hallway. "Wasn't that cop using your computer earlier today?"

"He was playing Sudoku, Jimmy, that's all."

"And you believe him?"

Jimmy's comment irritated her. Yes, she did believe Clay. He wouldn't delete her files.

"He was poring over your computer for a long time."

"And how do you know what happened? Stu said you were tied up in traffic and couldn't make the editorial meeting."

"I got back earlier than expected. That's when I saw him at your desk. You're not seeing clearly, Violet. Pretty evident you're attracted to the guy. Your feelings are written all over your face."

She wrinkled her brow. No way.

"Did he tell you why he's in Missoula?"

To keep her from digging too deeply into Mafia business, which she wouldn't mention to Jimmy. Instead, she hedged. "He's working with the U.S. Marshals office to ensure organized crime doesn't get a foothold in this area." Not a lie, but not the whole truth.

"He deleted your files, Violet. You must have found information he doesn't want revealed. Are you sure he's working on the right side of the law?"

"Of course, I'm sure." At least she thought she was sure. "I'll ask him about the files after work tonight. Besides, I saved the folder to my flash drive. I must have deleted the copy on my hard drive."

Jimmy raised his brow. "Are you two dating?"

"Of course not. Clay rented a room from my neighbor, Bernice. She sometimes invites me over for dinner, that's all."

Why did she need to explain herself? If she wanted to see Clay, she could. Jimmy was a friend and nothing more. When she looked up, she realized he had a different take on their relationship.

"You and I have been *friends* for a long time, Jimmy." Violet wanted to get that across loud and clear. "I know we went out a couple times in college, and I always enjoy being with you."

His mouth twisted. "No reason to explain your actions, Violet. You're allowed to see whomever you want."

Allowed? Under normal circumstances, she'd call him on his choice of words.

"Clay and I are friends," Violet said. "End of story. We knew each other in Chicago."

Jimmy's expression wilted. "So, you've got a history."

Why couldn't he let the subject drop? Violet grabbed his arm. "Jimmy, lighten up, okay? Clay hasn't changed anything between us."

He glanced down at her hand, and while his face was void of expression, his eyes narrowed. "If you want to find out about your missing files, I'd question that cop. He's moved in across the street from you, now he's deleting files on your computer and watching you while you're at work. Wonder what will happen next? Everything might seem like a coincidence to you. But there's a common denominator and his name is Clay West."

Jimmy walked back to his desk. He grabbed his jacket off his chair and stormed out of the newsroom, taking the stairs instead of the elevator so he wouldn't have to pass her desk.

Had she just lost an old friend because of Clay?

Or was the problem with Jimmy brewing before Clay had ever come to town?

• • •

The afternoon proved uneventful after the hot-headed reporter stormed out of the newsroom. Clay followed Violet home from work. She parked in her garage then crawled into his car. They headed for the hardware store and picked up a part Bernice needed for her garbage disposal, as well as two sturdy dead bolts for Violet's doors.

On the way back, Clay parked in her driveway and checked her house, which was starting to become a routine. Once assured no one had entered her home, he joined her on the porch where she waited.

"Why don't you sleep at Bernice's house tonight?" Clay suggested. "I told you she's got room."

"I can't, Clay."

"Of course you can, but you're being Aunt Lettie again," he teased.

"You don't need to keep watch all night."

He held up his hand to stop her. "Let me do my job, okay?"

"Is . . . is that all this is? Just a job?"

He stared down at her, unsure of what to say. Standing this close made it hard to think straight. He was a cop from Chicago. A guy who grew up on the South side. Not the best of neighborhoods. He'd seen it all. More than she would ever know. Violet deserved better. She deserved someone closer to her age, a guy who came home every night and was never in the line of fire. White picket fences, a couple of kids that looked as beautiful as she did and church on Sunday.

Clay wasn't sure he could provide any of those things.

But he wasn't thinking correctly so, instead of giving her a spoken reply, he bent down and kissed her sweet lips.

A few hours later, he was still thinking about that kiss when he crawled out from underneath the kitchen sink when the doorbell rang.

"I'll get it." Bernice opened the door. "Why, honey, I'm so glad you can keep Clay company tonight. There's a speaker at the church. I thought Clay might be interested, but he said you two had work to do."

Washing his hands in the sink, Clay chuckled as the older lady chattered on. Much as he had appreciated her invitation to attend the program, he didn't want to push his luck. No telling what God might do if he stepped inside the sanctuary of a church. It had been too long. Thinking back, he realized the last time had been at his ex-wife's funeral.

Drying his hands on a paper towel, Clay turned just as Violet stepped into the kitchen. Her windblown hair swirled around her face. Cheeks colored by the cold and eyes that sparkled a greeting were every bit as inviting as the smile that curved across her lips.

The fresh smell of the outdoors sailed into the kitchen along with her. Without thinking, he reached for her hand and pulled her close, wrapping his arms around her.

Violet hesitated a moment before the stiffness he felt initially melted as she moved closer.

"You're cold," he whispered, inhaling the lemon scent of her shampoo.

She laughed and the vivacious sound made him giddy.

Bernice stepped into the kitchen, and Violet pulled free to hold the older woman's purse while Clay helped her with her coat.

"You certainly look pretty," Violet said, taking in Bernice's wool dress and matching jacket.

"Thank you, dear. Clay said the color brings out my eyes."

Violet threw him an approving glance and winked.

"Just so Leonard notices."

"Someone from church?" Violet asked.

"He moved here to be close to his daughter after his wife died." The older woman turned to Clay. "The casserole is in the oven. Salad's in the fridge. There's cake for dessert."

"Have you eaten?" Violet was confused.

"I had leftovers earlier. Leonard and I are

staying for the dessert after the program." Bernice glanced at Clay's tools on the counter. "How's the disposal?"

"Ready to use. Just remember, no potato peels."

"As I've said before, you're an answer to my prayers." Bernice squeezed his arm then took her purse from Violet and headed for the garage.

"That woman knows how to make a guy feel good," Clay said once Bernice left the house. "When I fix something around my own place in Chicago, I'm the only one who notices. Work on something here and Bernice turns it into an answered prayer."

"She's a dear lady who loves the Lord."

"Bernice doesn't mince words about you, either."

Violet raised her brow. "Meaning?"

"Meaning, she thinks you're one in a million. A prize catch, I believe was the phrase she also used."

Violet's cheeks pinked.

"She said you deserve someone special." Clay stared down at Violet, realizing too late he was only inches away from her. Surely she could hear the pounding of his heart.

She blinked and turned toward the oven, looking as confused with her emotions as he felt about his.

Glancing at his toolbox, Clay forced his

thoughts back on track. "After we eat, I'll install those dead bolts."

The meal was delicious, and Clay learned a bit of Missoula's history, including about Lewis and Clark who had come through the Missoula Valley in 1805.

After dinner, Clay left the dishes, wanting to install the dead bolts first. The stars twinkled overhead and the moon smiled down on them as they walked to Violet's house.

Carrying his toolbox in one hand, Clay reached for hers with the other. Their fingers entwined without hesitation as if they'd been created for that very purpose.

The world seemed focused totally on them. Chicago and the Martino Mafia family were half a continent away. Tonight Clay wasn't a cop. He was a guy falling in love with a beautiful woman.

Clay could see himself in this neighborhood, helping Bernice with her repairs and spending lots of time with Violet. Missoula was a nice town, a place to settle down and live the good life.

Violet handed him the key to her house. He unlocked the front door and she followed him into the dimly lit living room, where both of them shrugged off their coats.

"I'll make coffee," Violet said, heading for the kitchen.

Flipping on another light, he turned and slipped back into cop mode. "Violet?"

She glanced at him over her shoulder, her eyes twinkling with happiness. Laughter escaped her lips, the buoyant sound in stark contrast to the cold chill that had slid over his portion of the room.

He pointed to the other side of the living room. Drawers had been pulled from her desk. Papers lay scattered over the floor. A lamp had overturned, and books from a shelf had been tossed into a pile on a nearby area rug. Her phone sat on the otherwise bare desktop.

Confusion swept across her face as Clay stated the obvious. "This time it's definitely the mob."

TEN

Violet's stomach roiled and she felt light-headed. "Clay—"

He reached out and steadied her, wrapping her in his arms.

Her sternum felt like a brick weight, collapsing her lungs.

"Easy, honey," he soothed, rubbing his hands over her back.

She gasped for air as hot tears stung her eyes. Clay had been right all along. The mob had been after her. Why had she been so foolish not to admit it to herself?

Because of what had happened with Aunt Lettie, of course. But she couldn't explain that to Clay.

Gathering strength, she pulled from his embrace. She needed to inventory her things and determine what had been taken.

Glancing at the empty desktop and at the clutter on the floor, realization hit. "My laptop's gone."

"Don't touch anything," Clay warned. "Stay here while I check the house."

He moved from room to room as she tried to comprehend what had happened. Had the intruder been after her computer when he'd broken in Monday night? And what about her files at work? Had someone accessed them or had she accidentally deleted them herself?

All this time, Violet hadn't wanted to admit Clay was right. She *had* placed herself in danger.

"The rest of the house looks okay. He must have found what he was looking for," Clay said, returning to the living room. "Who has a key?"

Violet tried to think. "Jimmy did when I first moved back to Missoula."

"Jimmy?" Clay raised his brow.

"He helped me paint the place while I stayed at Bernice's. Sometimes he'd get here earlier than I could, so I gave him a key. He gave it back before I moved in."

"Easy enough to make a copy."

She wrapped her arms around her waist, willing herself to be strong. "Jimmy wouldn't do that."

"You're too trusting, Violet. Jimmy's interested in everything about you. Have you noticed anything out of place or missing before this?"

"No, of course not."

Clay was right. Jimmy wanted their relationship to develop into something longterm, but he'd never overstepped the bounds of propriety and he'd never verbalized his feelings.

"We need to report the break-in to the police." Clay pulled out his cell. "While they're on the

146

way, check your valuables and ensure nothing else has been taken."

Her missing files once again came to mind.

Clay narrowed his eyes. "There's something you're not telling me." She explained about the files on her work computer.

"Why didn't you mention it?"

She looked into his eyes, feeling she had betrayed him with her earlier reticence. Her mistrust of law enforcement continued to get in the way. "I . . . I—"

He sighed. "It's okay, Violet. I know you're still not sure you can trust me."

Tears stung her eyes. He was right, just as he'd been about the danger.

"Was everything deleted on your computer at work?"

At least he hadn't lingered on the trust issue.

"Only the documents concerning the Chicago Mafia. Luckily, I backed up the information on to my flash drive."

"Which is where?"

She hesitated.

He held up his hands. "Don't tell me. I'll call the police from the kitchen and give you privacy to ensure it's still safe."

"No, Clay, it's okay." She dug in her purse and was relieved to find the tiny flash drive where she'd placed it earlier.

He made the call, explained what had happened

and requested Officer O'Reilly be notified.

"O'Reilly's off duty tonight, but a patrol car's in the area," Clay said, closing his phone. "An officer will be here soon."

Violet moved through her house, checking the few valuables she had. Nothing in the bedroom appeared to have been touched. A tiny cross necklace that had belonged to Aunt Lettie remained in the velvet-lined box on her dresser.

She returned to the living room just as Clay opened the front door. He motioned the officer inside and quickly explained about everything that had happened, including the missing laptop and the problem with her files at work.

Tall, with short blond hair and blue eyes, the officer seemed both efficient and sympathetic.

"So, you're the guy who helped us bring in Jamie Favor?" The cop was impressed.

Clay nodded. "O'Reilly said he divulged the name of a drug dealer in the neighborhood."

"We pulled him in last night. Hopefully, things will quiet down around here now."

The officer turned to Violet. "What's on your laptop, ma'am? Bank records? Online financial accounts?"

She shook her head. "I do all my financial transactions in person at the bank."

"Are you working on any stories someone may not want written?"

She looked at Clay before she answered. "I'm

currently doing a story on the need for increased police officers in the city." She didn't mention the missing information on the Mafia.

The cop nodded his approval. "Thanks for being on our side. We've got enough folks who don't appreciate what we do."

Violet felt a stab of conscience. The officer seemed like a decent man. Stu had probably been right to reject the first story she'd submitted about the local P.D. Her prejudice against the chief of police due to what had happened back home in Granite Pass had more than colored her reporting. She had made a mistake and let her personal feelings sway the story. Something any good reporter shouldn't have allowed to happen.

"No sign of forced entry," the officer said after he checked the house. "Someone must have made a copy of your key. I'll talk to the lock-smiths in the area and your neighbors to see if they noticed anything. Have your locks changed in the morning."

"I plan to do that," Violet said.

"Does anyone have a spare key?" the officer asked.

The same question Clay had posed. Cops must think alike. She didn't want Jimmy involved. Besides, she'd given him the key almost a year ago. Why would he choose to enter her house now?

Quinn's warning played through her mind.

Jimmy had access to her computer at work. Would he sabotage her Mafia story in order to help his own career?

"What about someone at work?" Clay prompted as if reading her thoughts.

"No one has a key," she said with conviction.

Clay's face was hard to read. She prided herself in being a good judge of character. Jimmy had been a friend for years. Nothing had changed.

Except Clay had entered the picture.

The officer did a thorough search of the exterior of the house, looking for any sign of entry. He fingerprinted the doors, as well as the areas that had been disturbed inside.

"We'll increase patrols in the area," the officer said once he had finished. "I'll let O'Reilly know, and contact you if we uncover any leads."

When the officer left, Clay reached for his tool kit. "After I install the dead bolts, you're coming back with me to Bernice's house."

Violet packed a small overnight bag as Clay worked. Where had she gone wrong? Had Gwyn's boyfriend discovered she'd been passing information? Or had Violet's search for information about the two murdered green-eyed women been her own undoing?

What about Clay? His actions had adversely affected a sting the police had planned in Chicago.

A slipup on his part. But what if he had purposefully tried to thwart the operation? Could he be something other than a good man focused on justice and the rule of law?

Christ preached forgiveness, although it was a message Violet sometimes struggled to embrace. The board of inquiry was looking into Clay's actions. Their ruling would decide his future and reveal the truth. Until then, she'd have to rely on her inner compass, and right now it was saying Clay was an honest man.

Hopefully, her compass was true and not wrapping her in a false sense of security.

Clay installed the dead bolts without problem. They were top-of-the-line and would provide additional protection for Violet.

She turned worried eyes toward him as they left her house and locked the doors behind them. If she had refused to spend the night at Bernice's house, Clay would have camped out on Violet's front porch. Despite the cold, he had to keep her safe. Right now, he enjoyed the warmth of her hand and the way her fingers wrapped through his. A nice fit.

"It's going to be okay, Violet," he encouraged, giving her hand a gentle squeeze. "If the perpetrator left prints, the cops will take him down."

She flashed him a tenuous smile. "Thanks for not saying 'I told you so.'"

"I'd never say that." He dropped her hand and

moved his arm around her shoulders, drawing her close. Her perfume teased his nostrils. He tilted his head toward hers. At that moment, the night didn't seem so cold.

He was almost disappointed when they arrived at Bernice's home. Violet stepped out of his embrace so he could unlock the door.

"I still have some work to do on the story that's due tomorrow." She stepped into the home. "Would you mind if I use your laptop?"

"Why don't you make a pot of coffee while I get my computer booted up and online?"

Clay placed his laptop on the dining table so Violet could work. Even if the Mafia had the information on her laptop, she was still in grave danger.

Someone had gotten into her home unnoticed twice. The next time might be to do something far worse, and that's what worried Clay. He couldn't let her out of his sight, yet as determined as Violet was to make her own path through life, keeping the headstrong reporter safe might be a hard task to accomplish.

The smell of fresh-perked coffee filled the air as Violet inserted her flash drive into Clay's laptop. With a few taps on the keyboard, her e-mail provider popped on to the screen. She entered her password and found a new message in her mailbox.

Clicking on the subject line, an e-mail from Gwyn appeared on the screen.

Did you locate Jen Davis?

Violet wrote a hasty reply, explaining what she and Clay had found in Billings.

The U.S. Marshals are looking for Jen. They'll keep her safe. They can help you, too, if you're willing to accept their protection.

Gwyn's reply came quickly.

I'll call you soon.

Violet closed her e-mail as Clay came into the dining area, carrying two mugs of coffee. He pulled out a chair and sat next to her while she told him about the message she'd just received.

"Did you mention Micah's offer?"

Violet placed her cell on the table. "She said she'd call me." Before Violet had finished her coffee, her cell rang. Relief swept over her when she heard Gwyn's voice.

"Tell me what you found out?" the woman asked.

"I talked to a U.S. Marshal today," Violet said. "He'll be able to get you into Witness Protection and set you up in another city."

153

"What about Ruby Maxwell and Carlie Donald? No one kept them safe."

"Do you know if they contacted someone from their past? That could have led the mob to their doors."

"My boyfriend never mentioned how the mob found them. They probably didn't realize their lives were in danger."

How many other women in Witness Protection were in danger, as well?

"You'll have to cut all ties, Gwyn. You won't be able to talk to family or friends you knew in Chicago."

"I'm all alone, Violet. That won't be a problem."

"If you're willing to provide evidence against the mob, the Marshals will get you to safety."

Violet thought once again of Jen Davis and the strange man who had appeared wherever they went in Billings, as well as the vehicle that had almost crashed into Clay's car. Hopefully, the Marshals would find Jen before the mob did.

Violet looked at Clay. His eyes were filled with concern. "Tell me where you're staying, Gwyn. I've got a friend who's a cop. We'll come and get you." She reached out her hand and squeezed Clay's. "He'll keep you safe."

"I'm still worried someone's following me. Once I feel secure enough, I'll contact you so we can meet."

A sense of foreboding settled over Violet when she disconnected and glanced once again at Clay. Despite the way she felt about law enforcement, she had to trust Clay. Violet had promised never to reveal her informant's name, but Gwyn needed protection. Clay would notify the Marshals, who could take her to a safe house.

Clay had protected Violet. He would get Gwyn the protection she needed, as well.

"It's time I give you all the information about my informant. Her name's Gwyn Duncan." Violet opened her cell phone. "I took this picture of her at the coffee shop."

Clay glanced at the photo then dug in his pocket for his own cell and pulled up almost the identical picture that he had taken of Gwyn.

"Why didn't you show Micah the photo this morning?" she asked.

Clay's gaze warmed her. "I knew you'd provide everything once you could trust me."

Violet's lips trembled and tears stung her eyes. Why had she doubted Clay?

He pulled her into his arms, and she felt the strength of his embrace.

She'd asked God to help her protect women caught in the grip of organized crime. He had sent her Clay.

Jen Davis, Gwyn Duncan, Olivia Jensen and Eloise Hill were being hunted by the Chicago mob. Eloise's daughter, Kristin, might also be in danger.

Dear God, keep them safe.

Violet snuggled closer.

Keep Clay safe, as well.

ELEVEN

Once Violet refocused her attention on the story she needed to write, Clay stepped into the kitchen and called Jackson, filling him in on the information about Gwyn.

"Did Micah tell you about Jen Davis, who might be in danger?"

"Jen Davis? Young woman, green eyes, Witness Protection, Montana, and currently unaccounted for? Yeah, Micah called me after you and Violet met with him this morning. Sounds like it ties in with the two Montana murders."

"There's another problem."

"Yeah?"

"Someone broke into Violet's house and ransacked her office area. Her laptop's gone."

"Sounds like the mob's found her for sure. If they've got her laptop, they must have the information she collected for that story she wants to write about the Martino family and the Montana murders."

"The mob will sit on the information, but if someone else stole her laptop, we still might see the story in print."

"Is there something you haven't told me, Clay?"

"Duplicate files about the Mafia were deleted from her computer at work. We had talked about the mob having a go-to guy in Missoula. Probably the man I chased from her house the night I arrived. There's a lot of back-and-forth movement of people through the newspaper office. Violet's desk sits in a corner by the elevator. I walked in this morning, and everyone was tied up in a meeting."

"I'll call the paper's editor and have him send me a list of the folks on staff. Wouldn't hurt to check them out."

Exactly what Clay had planned to do until Violet objected.

"What else is she working on? Any other stories that might play into the mix?"

"Other than the Mafia story? She's doing a feature on the local police force."

"I hope she paints the cops in a good light."

After her reaction to Chief Howard, Clay wasn't sure how Violet would slant the story.

"Is she safe tonight?" Jackson asked.

Clay glanced into the dining room. "She's okay for now. Tomorrow she's having new locks installed on her house. I plan to stay around for a few more days."

"Good man. Keep me updated."

"Will do."

Clay flipped his cell closed as the back door

opened and Bernice breezed into the kitchen. "I'm home."

She slipped her coat from her shoulders and hung it in the closet. "The program was wonderful."

"And your new friend?" Violet asked as she rose from the table.

"Leonard? Such a gentleman." Bernice glanced at Clay. "He reminds me of you. Older, of course. But a good man."

The same words Jackson had used. He'd never thought that particular phrase applied to him. Determined. Dedicated, maybe. But good?

Being with Leonard had added a new bounce to Bernice's step and an enthusiasm in her voice Clay hadn't noticed earlier. He hated to spoil the moment by telling her about the break-in. "Maybe I should meet this guy and check him out."

"You'd like him for sure. It's his inner goodness that attracted me to him in the first place. That's the part that reminds me of you, Clay."

She called into the dining room. "Violet, don't you see that goodness in Clay?"

"You're right, Bernice." Violet's eyes twinkled. "There is goodness in Clay, although I doubt he realizes how much."

Usually he could control his expressions, but his face burned with embarrassment. "How was the program?" he asked.

"A sad story with a triumphant ending. A man whose adult daughter had been murdered. He'd finally been able to forgive the murderer who was eventually brought to justice. The father felt the Lord's healing forgiveness. He went to the jail and talked to the young man about Christ's mercy and has written a book about how God changed both their hearts." Bernice pulled a small paperback from her purse and laid it on the counter. "He autographed a copy for me."

Clay glanced at the book. He'd never forgotten how Eloise, back at the foster home, talked about God taking the bad part of our lives and making something good come from it. The story of the father's forgiveness sounded like an example of the way Christ worked.

Violet stepped into the kitchen. "Care for some coffee and dessert, Bernice?"

"I've already had more than my limit following the program. A number of the ladies baked. But let me cut the cake for you two."

Bernice busied herself preparing two plates, while Violet refilled their coffee cups. As they ate, Violet and Clay told Bernice about the break-in and stolen laptop.

"You have to be careful, dear." Bernice patted Violet's shoulder. "I've worried about you being alone. Sometimes I don't think you use enough caution, coming home late like you often do."

She stretched her other hand toward Clay.

"Nice to know Clay's here to keep you safe."

Violet smiled at him. She didn't counter Bernice's comments. Instead, she winked, sending a buzz of energy rippling through him.

"I've got a third bedroom, Violet," the older woman continued. "You're staying here until all this calms down."

"I'm having my locks changed in the morning, Bernice."

"I won't take no for an answer." After chatting for a few more minutes, Bernice said good-night and headed for her bedroom.

Clay took a sip of his coffee and glanced at Violet over the rim of his cup. "You know when I first arrived in Missoula, I felt we were working on opposite sides."

"I did seem a bit anticop back then, didn't I?" Violet admitted.

"Because . . . ?"

She shook her head. "It's a long story. What about you? Did you follow in your dad's footsteps?"

Was her comment telling? Reading between the lines, Clay wondered if her negative feelings toward law enforcement had something to do with her dad. A subject he'd explore at a later time. Right now he needed to answer her question.

"My dad worked construction. Mom waited tables at a local restaurant. They were hardworking folks, trying to survive."

"I'm sure they were proud of you, Clay."

He shrugged. "They died when I was thirteen. Don't know if I'd done anything to earn their pride by that point."

"Then you went to the foster home where you met Eloise."

"That's right." He glanced at the doorway through which Bernice had just passed. "Eloise talked about the same things Bernice did tonight. God's mercy and love. Forgiveness was the stumbling block for me. I questioned why God had allowed my parents to die. Folks said He'd called them home. For a kid, it's hard to rationalize why a so-called loving God would leave a kid orphaned."

"Forgiveness is always hard." Sounded as if Violet struggled with that virtue, as well.

After loading the dessert plates into the dishwasher, Violet returned to the computer while Clay checked to ensure the doors were locked and added another log to the fire. Soon the wood crackled, warming the room from the winter chill.

He picked up the book Bernice had brought home, pausing occasionally as he read to glance at Violet. She focused on the computer, pounding the keyboard and scrolling through the files she accessed with her flash drive. Opening her purse, she pulled out a few typed pages and referred to them occasionally as she worked.

Clay was deeply moved by the story he read. The author recounted turning his heart to the Lord and, at long last, forgiving the man who had killed his only child.

"Do me a favor." Violet rose from the table. "Read what I've written and tell me what you think. Please?" She moved to the couch and sat near the fire, her hands outstretched to the warmth.

Clay placed the paperback on the coffee table near the Bible Bernice read each afternoon. Walking to the laptop, he sat in the chair Violet had just left and read her article.

Thought provoking and well written, the piece called for the city to fund additional monies to pay for an increase in police manpower. Violet made a good case for the need for more officers and outlined each person's civic responsibility to support their men in blue.

Her words warmed his heart. She had taken on the cops' cause and defended their standing in the community. Clay started to praise her work aloud when he realized she'd put her head on the arm of the couch and was sound asleep.

Violet's papers were scattered around the table. He noticed a story dated a few days earlier. Stu had scribbled *See me* followed by his last name on the upper margin.

Clay read the text. Again, Violet made an excellent point about the growing incidence of crime and the interstate and intrastate crime rings that were increasing their influence throughout Montana. She presented the facts in an orderly, convincing manner. Clay appreciated the points she made about needing more police coverage and the reasons for increasing the city budget. The only problem he found was when she mentioned the chief of police. At that point, her levelheaded reporting seemed skewed and so opposite what he'd read in the other sections of the feature.

His eyes glanced at the pile of papers, and he noticed a draft of another story. This one focused on the two women in Witness Protection murdered by the mob.

Clay's neck muscles tightened. If the story ever went to print, Violet would be at the top of the mob's most-wanted list. Surely, she still wasn't trying to sell the story to her editor.

He glanced at her sleeping on the couch. How much did he know about Violet? She'd earned a journalism degree and had excelled at UMT, winning the prestigious internship with the *Chicago Gazette*. A few folks on the paper had been forthright about Violet's need to prove herself and her desire for a permanent position on staff that never came through for her.

But Clay knew nothing about her family or what her life had been like growing up. Chief Howard had started his law-enforcement career in Violet's hometown. Clay checked the Missoula Police Department's home page and pulled up the chief's bio. His first job was in Granite Pass, a small town, two hours from Missoula.

Clay searched for a local Granite Pass newspaper and found a county publication that fortunately archived their issues. Following the prompts, he uncovered a list of articles.

The first he opened was a short piece about Everett Kramer, Violet's dad, graduating with a Bachelor of Arts in Education from the University in Montana. Clay did the math. Violet had been a kid, probably about seven years old.

The next article made his heart pound as he read the headline: *Kramer Last To See Murdered Girl Alive.*

Clay scanned the text. A high school senior's body discovered in a wooded area near the school . . . Everett Kramer had tutored the girl after school . . . person of interest . . .

Clay's fingers hit the next listing.

Second Victim Found . . . Lettie Kramer Dead.

Violet's aunt.

. . . body uncovered in shallow grave near highway . . . no suspects . . . Kramer family grieving . . . police questioned Everett Kramer through the night . . . no breaks in the case . . .

From what Clay pieced together, the police lacked enough evidence to level charges against

Violet's dad. No other arrests. Both cases remained unsolved.

Clay glanced again at Violet. Hard for a kid to go through life having her father suspected of being a murderer. Tongues wagged in small towns. *Innocent until proven guilty* wouldn't have prevailed.

Clay understood a little better why Violet pushed to protect the women in danger from the mob. She'd experienced firsthand the heartache of having a family member murdered. She'd probably had to prove herself, as well.

He unfolded the afghan Bernice kept on a nearby footstool and laid it over Violet. She snuggled down into the couch and sighed as he tucked the crocheted blanket around her shoulders.

Her curls spilled over the arm of the couch. His fingers touched the silky strands and smoothed them back in place. Her lips twitched into a smile, and in that instant, he knew he'd do anything to protect her.

Clay had read the author's words about forgiveness and a higher cause and how he had to embrace life with love and acceptance, but Clay hadn't let himself be free from the past. He'd guarded a part of his heart that had been broken when he was thirteen. The loss of his parents had affected him more than he'd ever allowed himself to realize.

Eloise had been a lifesaver when he needed something to hold on to lest he drown in his own pain, but she'd been only a temporary stopgap. He thought Sylvia would fill the void. But she'd had her own problems, and they'd been young. Neither supported the other constructively. Sacrificial love? Not at that time of his life.

If only he could have been more aware of her insecurity. She'd turned to drugs, which had been a crutch when she was a teen, before they'd met and married. He'd known she'd been in rehab, but they both believed she wouldn't slip back into addiction.

His long work shifts and the stress of having a husband in the line of fire was her excuse for needing pills to get through the day. At some point, she needed more than prescription drugs.

He'd encouraged her to go into rehab again, but she never found the strength to seek healing. Instead, she'd left him for a path of darkness and despair.

Clay's gut tightened at the memory of seeing her on a street corner one cold winter night. He'd stopped to help her. Spaced out on the drugs she'd bought with the money she earned selling her body, Sylvia had thought he was another john and started to get into his car.

When recognition lifted the cloud of her existence and she saw him clearly, Sylvia had run away into the night.

Clay never saw her alive again. His last memory was her face staring back at him from the morgue when he'd been called in to identify her body.

He dropped his head in his hands, trying to close out the memory. His gaze rested on the Bible and paperback, lying side by side. He'd just read about a father's mercy and the way forgiveness can heal the most hardened hearts.

Who did Clay need to forgive?

Sylvia? He'd done that already.

Cameron Trimble, the pimp who'd used her and abused her? The drugs he fed Sylvia had caused her death.

Forgive Cameron? Clay had had a different reaction when he'd seen him, yet vengeance wasn't cathartic or freeing. The beating meant Clay had more to forgive. Now he had to forgive himself. Sometimes that was the hardest thing to do.

What about God?

Clay shook his head. Old habits were tough to break. Clay had been mad at God for so long, he didn't know how to change his feelings.

If God were all loving, wouldn't He be the first to offer forgiveness? Until then, Clay would continue on the path he'd walked for so long.

Once again, he looked at Violet. Was she a gift from God? Or would she be taken from him like his parents, like Eloise, like Sylvia? His track record wasn't good.

No matter what had happened in the past, Clay had to protect Violet and keep her from publishing the article on the mob killings.

Clay's hand slipped to the Bible resting on the coffee table. Not knowing whether God was listening, he whispered, "Help me, Lord. I need to keep Violet safe."

TWELVE

Violet awakened on her neighbor's couch. Clay had kept the fire blazing and hunkered down on the overstuffed chair nearby, his nose glued to the book Bernice had bought at the church program.

He was the first person she saw this morning, smiling at her through tired eyes as he offered her a cup of coffee. A day's beard darkened his jaw and his tousled hair softened his expression. For once, he didn't appear totally in control and on top of things.

After a huge breakfast Bernice insisted on serving, Violet scurried home for a shower and change of clothes. She'd arrived at work ten minutes early, half-expecting to see Clay hanging around in the hallway. She'd told him she was working from the office all day and would be safe. Evidently, he believed her.

The first thing she did was send Stu an electronic copy of the article she had written on the police department. A hard copy now waited in his in-box. She made some corrections to the piece on the women in Witness Protection and saved the revisions to her flash drive. Hopefully, she could change Stu's mind, and he'd accept that article for publication, as well.

Gulping down the last of the bottled water Bernice had tucked in her lunch, Violet glanced at the photo on her desk of Aunt Lettie and her dad. Someday, she hoped information would come forward about the person who had taken Lettie's life.

For so long, she'd pushed and struggled to find answers. Maybe it was time to hand the case over to God. No doubt, He would deal with the killer whether He allowed Violet to know what had happened or not.

The phone on her desk rang. She pulled the receiver to her ear. "Kramer."

"Violet, it's Stu. Come to my office. I want to talk to you."

Not good. Stu usually wandered through the workplace and personally asked reporters to see him. Using the phone wasn't the way he routinely beckoned people to his office.

Violet grabbed a notepad and pencil, slipped her feet into the heels she'd discarded earlier and scooted her chair back from her desk. The sandwich she'd just devoured sat like a lump of coal in her stomach.

How bad could it be? Stu had counseled her on more than one occasion. He could fire her. Not an option she chose to embrace.

Focused on Stu's door, she didn't see Jimmy

standing outside Quinn's cubicle.

"Everything okay?" he asked as she neared.

She tried to smile.

"You look a little pale, Violet. Are you sure you're all right?" Jimmy's interest was questionable. She detected a smirk of satisfaction under his inquiring gaze.

"I'm fine," she insisted. Glancing into the cubicle, she spied Quinn at his computer. He, too, looked worried. Did he know something she didn't? And had he told Jimmy?

Her steps echoed in the now nearly silent newsroom. She felt a kinship with Marie Antoinette marching to the guillotine. Suppose Stu *did* fire her?

She could always move home and work on the country paper. Or perhaps talk to Ross Truett about getting a job on the *Yellowstone County Reader.*

Then she'd be back at square one. Low man in the stringer pool, writing fillers about ladies' groups and men's clubs and hunting and fishing and all the other human-interest pieces that filled the local rags.

Again, not the stories she wanted to write.

Bracing for the worst, Violet squared her shoulders. She would face her executioner with her head held high. No sniveling. No begging to keep her job.

Okay, maybe a little begging.

172

"You wanted to see me," she said stepping into Stu's office. He held the hard copy of her police article in his hands. She braced for the worst.

"The article you submitted . . ."

In her mind's eyes, she saw the sharp blade of the guillotine suspended above her head. The sound of falling metal seemed almost real.

Raising her hand to her throat, she swallowed. "Yes?"

"Nice job."

The guillotine screeched to a stop inches from its mark. She blinked.

"Excellent writing."

Excellent? Stu rarely spoke in superlatives. The lump in her stomach softened to molten gold. Her knees went weak. She'd take excellent.

"Thank you, sir."

"It'll run on tomorrow's front page. I'll probably assign you a follow-up later."

Before she turned toward the door, she saw the sunlight shimmer on the Clark Fork as bright as her mood after the current turn of events.

Trying not to giggle, she left Stu's office. The newsroom bustled with activity. No one noticed her exuberance or the elation that buoyed her step. Was she walking over the hardwood floor or floating?

Excellent! How 'bout that! Finally, a positive from Stu. Things were turning her direction for a change. Maybe the article on the murdered women would see the light of day after all.

Jimmy poked his head out of Quinn's cubicle as she passed. "Trying to one-up me." Once again, his smile lacked sincerity.

He couldn't have heard Stu. "One-upping you in what way, Jimmy?"

"Your article." He pointed to Stu's open door. "He looked pleased."

"I'm sure Stu's happy about your work, as well."

"Yeah, right."

Violet glanced around Jimmy and caught Quinn's eye. Pursed lips, creased forehead. His expression brought to mind his words of caution the other night. He'd mentioned Jimmy's desire to get ahead.

Maybe Quinn was right. Maybe she needed to be more careful around Jimmy.

She approached her desk, remembering the missing files. Jimmy had gone into her voice mail to retrieve Clay's message the night he'd arrived in Missoula. Had Jimmy gone into her files to read and then delete the information she had compiled on the Chicago Mafia? She was beginning to think Jimmy was anything but a friend.

Glancing into the hallway, Violet smiled as the elevator door opened and Clay stepped into the hallway. "Grab your coat and purse. We've got an appointment to talk with Chief Howard."

"About what?"

"Your aunt Lettie."

"Did you find out something about her murder?" Violet asked, hurrying to keep up with Clay as they left the Plaza Complex and headed to his car.

"You're a reporter, Violet. You deal with facts." He opened the passenger door and slammed it closed after her. She waited as he rounded the car and climbed behind the wheel.

"Cops investigate crime," he continued as he turned the key in the ignition. "They deal in facts, as well."

"So how's this involve my aunt?"

Clay pulled into the middle lane, heading for police headquarters. "Whatever happened when you were a child affects your view of law enforcement."

"I trust you, Clay. We talked about it last night."

"But you still have a problem with cops. Chief Howard was a rookie in your hometown. Let's see what he remembers about Lettie's death."

"There's nothing wrong with my memory, if that's what you're suggesting." She crossed her arms and stared straight ahead, wishing she'd stayed at the paper. What could the chief tell her that she didn't already know?

"Trust me. Okay?" Clay looked at her with

such sincerity that some of her resolve weakened. Could new evidence have come to light?

She'd listen to what the chief had to say—not that it would change what she knew to be true about her aunt's death. Even if the chief shed new information about the crime, Violet would still struggle with the cops.

She flicked a sideways glance at Clay. Present company excluded, of course.

Chief Howard stood and shook Clay's hand when they walked into his office.

"Good to see you, Violet." He motioned them toward two chairs that sat in front of his desk.

Clay got right to the point. "As I told you when I called you this morning, we want to talk to you about the murders in Violet's hometown and what the cops uncovered."

The chief nodded as he took his seat behind his desk. He gave Violet a long, hard look before he spoke. "Everett Kramer—Violet's dad—was a good man. Hard working. Trying to support his wife and daughter. After his parents died, he took in his kid sister. Lettie was pretty as a picture but headstrong."

"Stubborn," Violet clarified.

"Did she have a boyfriend?" Clay asked.

"Brad Meyer was his name." Violet thought back to the night Lettie had died. Her aunt had dabbed perfume on her neck and wrists and had let Violet dab her wrists, as well.

"Brad ran with a bad crowd," the chief explained. "We questioned him, but he had an alibi for both murders. A number of his friends had been picked up on possession a few nights before the first murder. Lettie claimed she'd seen someone drive away from the school with the girl on the afternoon the teen was killed."

Violet crossed her legs. "Not that anyone believed her."

The chief nodded. "Everyone thought she made up the story to protect her brother. Then Lettie ended up dead."

"Was the M.O. the same for both victims?" Clay asked.

Rubbing his jaw, the chief stretched back in his chair. "Both died from a broken neck. The teen's body was found in a clearing not far from her school. Lettie's body was uncovered near the main highway."

"My dad worked at the school the teen attended," Violet said. "He'd gone back to college and had made the long commute down here to UMT for a weekend-only program geared toward older students. Dad graduated that December and landed a long-term, substitute-teaching position in January that would have lasted until the end of school term."

The chief nodded in agreement. "Talk was he would have picked up a permanent position for the next year."

Clay held up his hand. "Let me guess, he lost his job after the girl's murder."

"You got it. My dad had tutored the teen the day she'd died and was the last person to see her alive."

"Except for the killer." Clay gave Violet an encouraging smile. "Were the two victims friends?"

"Lettie was nineteen," the chief said. "She ran with an older crowd. The younger girl's reputation wasn't lily-white. She'd been involved with a number of boys. Had a couple of parties at her house when her mom—a single parent—was out of town."

"Previous drug use?"

"Not that the police knew. And no signs of abuse or molestation."

"Did Lettie get a look at the guy driving the teen?"

The chief shrugged. "She was about thirty yards from the road when the car passed. She couldn't ID the driver, although she was sure it wasn't her brother."

Violet bristled. "So, it was guilt by association?"

The chief held up his hands. "You're jumping to the wrong conclusion. The Granite Pass cops were thorough."

Clay raised a brow. "Were they, Chief?"

Howard paused for a moment, then shrugged.

"Okay, they tried to intimidate Everett. But he refused to offer any additional information."

"Maybe he didn't know anything else about the case," Clay offered.

Chief Howard nodded. "Maybe."

"Lettie might have been killed because she'd seen the murderer. The perp could have been afraid she'd be able to recognize him?"

"That's certainly a possibility, Clay. In a way, discovering Lettie's body eased the suspicion on Everett. Seemed logical the same killer had committed both crimes. Everett and Lettie were close. Too much of a stretch to think he'd killed his sister. The wife and Lettie got along."

"I idolized her," Violet said.

"The Kramers had been the perfect little family until all this happened," the chief said.

Clay hesitated for a moment. "You seem pretty sure of how things went down that long ago, Chief."

A smile twisted his lips. He pulled a worn notebook from his desk. "I reviewed my notes after you called this morning. I was a new recruit fresh out of the Police Academy when the murders occurred. Although wet behind my ears, I was smart enough to know I had a lot to learn."

He patted the leather cover. "My staff calls me a detail man. My mother says I was born that way. I jotted down everything about the case in this little book."

"Any chance I could review your notes?"

"Why not?" The chief tossed the notebook into Clay's outstretched hand.

Not wanting to take more of the chief's time, Clay extended his right hand. "Thank you, sir, for the information."

"Been great talking to you, Clay." Chief Howard's handshake was firm, his smile encouraging. "You ever get tired of Chicago and want to settle down in our neck of the woods, let me know."

Sounded like the chief was offering him a job, which Clay appreciated. Although if the inquiry in Chicago decided against him, Clay doubted he'd find a job in law enforcement anywhere. He'd be banned from the work he loved just the way Violet's father had been banned from education.

Hard place for a man to be. Especially with a wife and daughter at home, needing to be fed. Tough times for the Kramer family had to have gotten worse.

Clay reached for the leather notebook as the chief shook Violet's hand. Maybe progress had been made after all.

"Let's get lunch," Clay said once they climbed into the car. They found a quiet sandwich shop and spent the next thirty minutes eating pastrami on rye and reading Chief Howard's notebook.

"Most times apprehending a perpetrator

180

requires common sense and endless hours checking details and running down leads," Clay explained. "Sometimes those who work a case are too close to see the obvious, and the very detail that should provide the solution can be inadvertently overlooked."

He called Jackson and asked him to circulate Lettie's boyfriend's name on the street. Hard to imagine anything would come of it, but crimes were solved sometimes in the most illogical ways.

Clay wanted to make everything better for Violet before he returned to Chicago. His gut tightened, knowing the longer he was around her, the harder it would be to leave.

After lunch, Clay dropped Violet at her office and spent the next few hours calling his own sources in Chicago. He'd worked undercover long enough to have a pulse on the Windy City. At least the South side.

Violet was dead set on protecting women in Witness Protection, so he sent out feelers to see what he could find. Although he told himself it was an afterthought, he also threw the name of Aunt Lettie's boyfriend into the mix. Jackson had his street sources. Clay knew others. Between them, if the guy had spent any time in Chicago, someone would know.

Clay's cell rang. He pulled it to his ear, surprised to hear Chief Howard's voice. "You need to know a bit more about Violet's past. I didn't want to tell you while she was in my office."

"Yes, sir." Clay waited for the chief to explain.

"Shame to see how the town acted toward the family. You would have thought they'd all been tried and convicted of the crime. As I mentioned, Everett—Violet's dad—lost the position at the school, and everyone knew he'd never get a job involving kids again. He couldn't find work. The family suffered, of course. Lettie's death compounded the situation. Financial problems and being ostracized by just about the whole town had to have taken its toll."

Clay thought of Violet. Only a child, but old enough to be aware of what had happened.

"When the local garbage hauler moved east, Everett rented a truck and started his own company. Must say, he's done well for himself."

"Has the town forgotten?"

"The family found acceptance in a small church community. The other folks in town? Hard to say. Violet inherited her father's go-it-alone characteristics. Either that or she'd been hurt too many times. Top of her class. Top in just about everything. Seemed she always had to prove herself."

Clay's heart went out to Violet. No wonder she fought to get ahead even now. Old habits were hard to break. She'd always been the odd man out. Never accepted by the other kids, the memory of the murder always hanging over her head.

By two o'clock, he was heading back to the Plaza Complex when he passed a floral shop. Women like flowers, and he and Violet had become partners, so to speak. They could celebrate their new working relationship over dinner tonight. The flowers would be a way to express his thanks. Violet finally seemed to realize Clay was here to help, not hinder her work.

Clay saw Violet as soon as he stepped off the elevator, and the ripple of excitement that passed through his body confirmed he was committed to their new relationship. Violet was more than a woman who needed protection. She had opened his eyes to other needs, as well. He'd caught himself, only this morning, thinking about settling down, perhaps starting a family. Thoughts that he'd pushed away for too long.

He stepped toward her and held out the bouquet. "Flowers for a beautiful lady." Corny, but he wasn't the best with words.

"How 'bout dinner tonight? Bernice said there's a new French restaurant. I can make reservations for seven or seven-thirty, depending on when you get off work."

"Oh, Clay, that sounds wonderful."

He smiled.

"But I already have plans."

His smile faded.

"A guy from college is coming into town."

Clay's euphoria vanished. "We'll do it another time."

"I could tell him I'm tied up," she offered.

"No reason to change your date." Jimmy was a college friend. How many guys did she have hanging around? "Just be careful and remember to lock your doors."

"Thanks again for installing those dead bolts."

"You used them when you left this morning, didn't you?"

"Of course."

"What about the locksmith? Have you contacted him?"

"It's on my list of things to do."

"Call me if you have any problems." Even if it involves the old boyfriend, Clay wanted to add. "It's none of my business, but this guy you're going out with, do you trust him?" Did Clay notice a moment of hesitation?

"Of course I trust him," Violet said with conviction. "Ross is a nice guy."

"Nice guys come in last," Clay muttered as he rode the elevator to the first floor and walked into the cold crisp winter air. Probably the surveillance he'd been pulling, but he felt tired.

Climbing into his car, he slammed the door. What was his problem? He shouldn't be upset because Violet was seeing someone. She was young and beautiful and deserved to find someone to love. She had her whole life ahead of her. Knowing about her aunt's death and the pain of loss she'd experienced as a child, Clay wanted only good things for Violet's future.

A cop wasn't a good security risk for a husband. Violet could do better. A lot better.

Clay had allowed his own emotions to get involved with his job. He should have focused on Violet's security issues instead of on her. She'd be at work for a few more hours. No reason for him to hang around. He'd return later to follow her home and make sure she remained safe.

Tonight, he'd reread the notebook the chief had given him in case he'd missed anything the first time through. Then he'd make a few more phone calls.

Clay might not be able to give Violet his undivided attention over dinner tonight, but he could give her what he was good at doing . . . finding the man who had killed her aunt.

THIRTEEN

Violet watched the elevator doors close behind Clay, angry with herself for agreeing to see Ross. No-chemistry Ross. One date. Would it hurt so much?

Of course it would. She wanted to be with Clay.

She smelled the flowers. Red roses from a no-nonsense cop. Not what she'd expected. But then, Clay West was full of surprises.

She found a vase, arranged the bouquet and placed it on her desk. Her eyes kept focusing on the flowers instead of her work. Finally, she checked her e-mail and found a message from Gwyn.

Let's try again. The sandwich shop in the Bryant Strip Mall at 5:30 p.m.

Violet looked up as Jimmy neared her desk.

"The cop got you flowers?"

"Pretty, aren't they?"

Jimmy shrugged and shuffled his feet as if he were a kid needing to get something off his chest. "I'm sorry for the way I've been acting recently."

She closed her e-mail and focused her attention on him.

"I wasn't eavesdropping, if that's what you thought earlier," he continued. "Quinn told me Stu was pleased with your work."

"Stu tells Quinn and Quinn tells you? Sounds like everyone's playing Gossip." She thought back to the game she'd played in her youth

This time Jimmy's smile was sincere. "Pretty silly, huh?"

"Tell me you had my best interest at heart, and I'll forgive you."

"I did, really, Violet. I've been worried about you going off in your own direction. Stu likes the staff to follow his lead. You were starting to usurp his control."

"Apology accepted," she said, wondering if his change of heart was sincere. Either way, she wanted to clear the air between them. Life was too short and the newspaper staff was too small a group to let petty disagreements get between them.

Her phone rang. She held up her hand as she pulled the receiver to her ear.

"Kramer."

"Violet, it's Ross. I'll be in town within the hour. How 'bout if I pick you up at your house about 7:00 p.m.? We can get something to eat. Maybe see a movie."

"Sounds great. See you at seven."

She hung up, noting Jimmy's raised brow.

"You and the cop going out tonight?" he asked, glancing at the roses.

She shook her head. "I told you there's nothing between us."

"Yeah, right." His tone had darkened.

"Violet?" Stu hurried toward her desk. "There's another story I need you to cover. An author whose daughter was murdered. He's written a book about forgiveness and is speaking at the library. Evidently, he was at one of the local churches last night where the city librarian heard the program. She asked him to talk to the Friday Reading Group today. Starts at 4:00 p.m."

Not the story she'd hoped to write, but she couldn't turn down an assignment. Especially with Stu's "excellent" still ringing in her ears.

Violet glanced at her watch. If she arrived at the library ahead of schedule, she'd be able to get a few quotes from the speaker before the program. Otherwise, she'd have to stay afterward. If he was signing his book, the line could be long, and she didn't want anything to keep her from meeting Gwyn at the appointed time.

Violet grabbed her coat and purse. Jimmy had walked back to his desk and was staring at her. The look on his face made her wonder if what he'd said earlier about their friendship had been true.

Quinn stuck his head out of his cubicle and waved to her, once again giving her a thumbs-up. His encouragement only served to underscore the negative vibes she got from Jimmy.

Clay had said she needed to be careful. Violet was starting to take his words to heart.

The program at the library took longer than Violet had expected. The man's story had been both poignant and uplifting, as Bernice had recounted last night. When his daughter had been murdered, the father knew the trauma and pain could draw him closer to God or drive them further away. He had worked hard to ensure God came first. The biggest test of God's unconditional love working in his life had been when he'd forgiven his daughter's killer.

His testimony had visibly touched many in the audience. Tears had swelled in Violet's eyes, and she'd choked back a lump that filled her throat.

For so long, she'd wanted to find Lettie's murderer, but she'd never thought about what she might be called to do once he'd been identified. Forgiveness hadn't entered the picture.

Something to ponder when she had time. Right now, she was late for her meeting with Gwyn. Violet raced to the strip mall on the southern edge of town. Not an area she often frequented. Pulling into the parking lot, she stomped on the emergency brake and yanked the key from the ignition.

Purse in hand, Violet ran toward the sandwich shop located on the far edge of the complex.

Night was falling, and the light from inside spilled out into the darkness.

She reached for the door handle and pulled, but the door failed to open. Shoving her face against the glass, she looked inside. No customers. No cooks. No waitresses.

Violet stepped back and glanced at the hours-of-operation sign hanging in the window.

Open 10:00 a.m.—5:00 p.m.

Where was Gwyn?

Violet swiveled around to stare at the parking lot. Was she waiting for her there? Violet searched for a brown-haired woman, whose picture she carried in her cell phone before returning to her own car. A shiver tingled her neck as if she could feel eyes watching her. Clay's words of caution once again rang through her mind. She missed the sense of security she always felt when he was near.

Earlier, she'd worried about Jimmy, but standing in the parking lot in the darkening night, Violet realized she should be worrying about a lot more than a guy from college.

Climbing behind the wheel, Violet checked her cell phone. If only Gwyn would call. If she were in danger, Violet could help. Clay would contact Micah, and the Marshals could get her the protection she needed.

Driving back to her house, Violet thought over everything that had happened. Once again, she had gone off on her own, trying to right the wrongs done to so many women, and she'd ended up not helping anyone.

Clay had warned Violet about sticking her nose into the Chicago Mafia's business. She'd ignored his warnings due to her own willful stubbornness. The Mafia was in Missoula. The two towns where the women had been killed weren't far away by Montana standards. The thugs could have driven to Missoula easily enough, especially if they got wind of a nosy reporter who was making trouble for the mob.

Tears stung Violet's eyes more from anger than anything else. Anger at herself for charging headlong into something that called for caution. She wanted to tell Clay she'd been wrong. In fact, she wanted to be with him tonight instead of Ross.

There was no comparison between the two men. Ross was a nice guy, but not the right guy for her. Clay got under her skin in a good way. He was exciting and energetic and full of life. She'd been attracted to him the first time she'd seen him in Chicago. No matter what she told herself, she was attracted to him even more now.

At the next red light, she plugged in Ross's cell number. When he didn't answer, she left a message. "Tonight's not going to work out, Ross. I'm tied up and won't be able to go out with you."

Seeing her house in the distance, Violet turned into the alleyway and parked in the garage. She'd try to contact Ross again. Then she'd order Chinese, head to Bernice's and surprise Clay for a change.

She smiled, feeling a sense of relief as she hurried toward her back door. She stuck her house key in the lock, realizing she'd never called the locksmith. Nor had she secured the dead bolt when she'd raced to her car this morning.

Silly woman, she told herself, pushing the kitchen door open and stepping inside. Throwing her purse on the table, she checked the time and hurried to the bedroom. She'd shower and change into jeans and a sweater and low shoes before she ordered the Chinese.

When she entered her bedroom, her heart crashed against her ribs. She reached for something, anything to steady herself. Her eyes blurred. A discarded tube of lipstick, the end caked and worn, lay on her white carpet.

Her stomach roiled, and the room swirled around her. The cold hand of fear clasped down on her throat, making her gasp for air as she read the message scrawled across the wall.

Roses are red, violets are blue, women have died and so will you.

FOURTEEN

Violet grabbed her purse and ran from the house. Keys in hand, she started her car, wanting to get as far away as possible from the message written across her bedroom wall.

She needed arms to hold her. She needed Clay.

Her phone rang. She dug into her purse.

"Clay?"

"Violet?" A woman's voice.

"Gwyn?"

"I'm leaving town. They've found me."

"Who's they?"

"Someone from Chicago."

"I'm in my car," Violet said. "Tell me where you are, and I'll meet you."

"I'm packing. I only have a few minutes."

"Are you near the sandwich shop?"

"Two blocks east. Take a left at the third light past the strip mall. There's an extended-stay motel on the right. I'm in room 103, in the rear, bottom floor."

"Give me ten minutes."

Violet stepped on the gas. She had to get there and convince Gwyn before she left Missoula for good that Witness Protection would be the best way to escape the mob.

Fumbling with her phone, Violet tried to plug in Clay's number while she drove, her foot pushing the accelerator to the floorboard. She entered an incorrect sequence of digits, irritated when a recording indicated her error.

Letting out a frustrated breath, Violet searched the road ahead. A dump truck approached in the oncoming lane. Dropping her phone to her lap, Violet clutched the wheel with both hands, navigating a tight curve, going faster than the limit. The tires screeched as she tried to hold the road.

The Mini slid across the yellow center line.

Letting up on the gas, Violet pulled back into her lane barely missing the oncoming truck. The startled driver laid on his horn, the sound bellowing through the night.

"Sorry!" Violet called out, knowing he couldn't hear her apology.

The muscles in her neck tightened. Her fingers burned from gripping the wheel. A straight stretch of road loomed ahead. No oncoming cars.

Once again, she reached for her cell, her fingers stiff and clumsy. The small cellular device slipped from her hand and dropped to the floor.

She moaned. Keeping her eyes trained on the road, she reached down with her right hand and slapped the floor. Where was the phone?

More cars approached. She straightened, needing both hands on the wheel.

Swish. Swish. Swish. Headlights flashed as they passed in the night.

Another car approached. High beams. Momentarily blinded by the glare, Violet flipped her own lights to high then lowered them to signal the driver.

He didn't get the message.

The glare of the headlights blinded her.

She blinked at the sudden darkness once the car had passed.

An overhead traffic light swayed in the wind ahead.

Red.

Violet slowed, glanced right and then left. No oncoming cars. Shoving her foot down on the gas, she powered through the crossing.

Arriving at the motel, Violet pulled behind the building. The trip from her house had taken eight minutes. Record time.

She pulled the key from her ignition and grabbed the cell she now spied lying near the brake pedal.

Racing from her car, she found room 103, knocked twice and, when no one answered, turned the knob.

The door creaked open.

"It's Violet."

Darkness greeted her. She stepped inside.

Smelled copper.

Something wet underfoot.

Violet flipped on the light.

Reaching for the door, she retched. The woman whose picture she'd taken two days ago lay in a pool of blood, her throat cut, her eyes open and a look of terror frozen on her face.

Trembling, Violet raised her cell phone and snapped a photo then, turning toward the door, she called 911.

Before the connection completed, a noise sounded behind her. Violet started to turn. Hands wrapped around her throat.

"Ruby and Carlie and Gwyn had to die. I tried to warn you, but you wouldn't listen. You messed with the mob. Now you'll die, too."

A car door slammed.

She screamed.

"Violet?" Clay's voice.

The hands slipped from her neck. She dashed for the door and stumbled outside. Clay pulled her into his arms.

Sobbing, she clung to him, feeling safe in his embrace. She couldn't think, couldn't react.

Another woman had died.

"Help me, Clay. The mob. They killed her. Tried to kill me."

Sirens sounded. A patrol car pulled to the curb.

Clay pointed two blue suits toward the motel

room. Two more officers appeared. "Circle to the rear. Cover the exit in back."

Clay held Violet's shoulders and stared into her eyes. "Are you all right?"

She nodded. "The killer was behind me. He . . . he whispered in my ear. His hands around my neck." She touched her bruised flesh.

The memory of Gwyn's body burned through her mind. In a moment of clarity, Violet realized if Clay hadn't arrived, she would have been the next to die.

Investigating crime scenes was a way of life for a cop in Chicago. Clay had developed a tough skin and a sense of detachment that had kept him from being affected by what he saw.

Until now.

This time he was too close, too involved. He couldn't separate his heart from what his head kept telling him. Violet had almost died. The mob had found her. If he'd arrived seconds later, he wouldn't be watching as she gave her statement to the officer in charge.

Clay called Jackson. "Another Montana murder."

"Not Violet?"

"Her informant from Chicago. The woman tried to escape her Mafia boyfriend. Someone followed her to Missoula."

"What about Violet?"

Clay's stomach tightened. "She evidently surprised the murderer."

"Did she see him?"

"Negative. He grabbed her from behind." Clay's mouth went dry. He swallowed, needing to give Jackson more information, and glanced again at Violet as if to ensure she was still alive. "The guy's message was 'Mess with the mob and you'll die.' "

"But she got away."

"Thank God, I arrived in time." Clay paused, his mind again playing tricks on him. He saw Violet lying on the floor in place of the victim.

Rubbing his free hand over his jaw, Clay willed the thought to flee. He needed to separate his feelings for Violet from his need to analyze the evidence or he'd compromise his ability to keep her safe.

"The killer heard me approaching and released her. Luckily, I had called Missoula P.D. when I arrived at the motel, just in case. Two patrol cars were in the area. The killer exited through a back door that spilled into the swimming-pool area. A side archway led to an empty lot. He probably had his vehicle parked there."

"Surveillance cameras?"

"They've been pulled and are being reviewed."

"Anything yet?"

"One man moving through the pool area. He wore a baseball cap and a hooded sweatshirt and kept his back to the cameras. The surrounding area is being canvassed. Cops are going door-to-door. Chief Howard's providing as much manpower as he can to track down every lead. FBI arrived a few minutes ago."

Jackson sighed. "I'll see if there's any talk on the street here in Chicago. Most of these lower-level mobsters like to brag about what goes down."

"Any activity around the Martino compound?"

"Not that we've seen. Salvatore might hang on for a while longer. Doubt we'll see many changes until he's gone."

"Once Missoula P.D. identifies the victim, see what you can find on her Mafia boyfriend. First name Angelo. Gwyn told Violet he wasn't high on the Mafia food chain. Despite that, Gwyn had good intel."

"Which she could have gotten from some of the other girls who serviced the mob. Sounds like they stick together."

"A sisterhood of support."

"I'll call you when I've got Violet at the safe house."

Flipping his cell closed, Clay glanced once again at the motel. Crime-scene tape cordoned off the sidewalk leading to Room 103.

Part of him wanted to scream with rage to the heavens for putting her in danger. The other part of him wanted to thank the Lord for allowing him to see her car swerve out of the alleyway.

He'd followed, and tried to call Violet's cell, but he kept getting her voice mail.

She'd driven at breakneck speed. He would have caught up with her, except for a red light and two approaching vans coming from opposite directions.

Thankfully, he'd stopped. As the vans had passed, he'd seen Baby On Board signs and little heads in car seats.

Once the intersection cleared, he'd taken off again, spying Violet's taillights in the distance.

He'd lost her again just before the motel appeared on his right. Weighing his options, he'd selected the extended stay as a possible destination.

A cop's instinct or a higher power? He'd never believed in divine intervention, but no matter what had caused him to head for the rear of the building, he was grateful.

Clay was equally grateful he'd programmed the Missoula police number into his cell and that two patrol cars had been in the vicinity.

The officer in charge nodded to Clay when he finished questioning Violet. "I've got everything I need."

Violet sat in the passenger side of his car with the motor running and the heater pumping warm air. Ashen faced, wide-eyed, she fidgeted with the buttons on her jacket.

The medical examiner had arrived, and the ambulance was waiting to remove the victim once the officer in charge released the body. Clay wanted Violet out of the area before the body bag rolled to the waiting wagon.

One of the officers approached. "Sir, we're almost finished with the crime scene. Chief Howard will be here shortly. You're free to leave, he'll contact you after he's finished here."

"What about her house?"

"We've got a team there, as well."

"And Ross Truett?" Violet had provided his name. Every option needed to be covered.

"He checked into a downtown hotel earlier today. No one has seen him since then."

"The chief has my number. Tell him to call me if he needs more information."

Clay slipped into the driver's seat and reached for Violet's hand. "We're going someplace safe." He needed to reassure her.

She looked at him with troubled eyes. "What about Gwyn?"

"They're finishing up the crime scene. Her body will go downtown."

"She doesn't have immediate family. Maybe a distant relative."

He rubbed his fingers over her hand. "The cops know what they're doing, Violet. They'll locate her next of kin."

She swallowed and glanced down at her lap

201

as if processing what he'd just said. Shock manifested in different ways. Hopefully, she'd be able to move beyond the trauma she'd seen tonight. For all her attempts to be strong, Violet had been deeply affected by finding the murdered woman. Who wouldn't be? Innocent women shouldn't die at the hand of a barbarian mobster.

Clay circled Violet with his arm and pulled her into his embrace. He wanted to hold her and keep her safe and ensure no one ever hurt her again.

He'd promised he'd keep her safe.

But he hadn't succeeded.

Now he had to work to find out who had done this terrible crime and who might still want Violet dead.

She huddled in his arms as he stared into the night. The killer was out there, waiting for Clay to lower his guard, waiting for Violet to be vulnerable once again.

Clay couldn't make another mistake.

FIFTEEN

The safe house was nicely decorated, and the older couple who lived there had done everything to ensure Violet's comfort for which she was grateful. A guest bedroom with bath in the rear of the home would provide privacy while FBI agents kept watch outside.

Sitting on the couch with the logs crackling in the fireplace seemed surreal. So much had happened. Violet blamed herself and her need to track down information about the mob.

"Heavy cream and two sugars." Clay held the mug out to her.

She tried to smile appreciating his concern. "Did you tell Bernice where I am?"

"Only that you were safe. Not your whereabouts."

"She can be trusted, Clay."

He raised his brow. "No one knows where you are."

"What about the paper? I've got another story to write." She knew the answer before Clay explained yet again how everything was on hold until they found out who had killed Gwyn. The unspoken reality was they might never find the murderer.

Violet glanced around the small home. As much as she appreciated the people who had taken her in, she felt confined. "Twenty-four hours. That's as long as I'll remain in hiding."

"Violet, please, work with me for a change."

She pulled the mug to her lips and tried to still the turmoil within her.

Clay's cell chirped. He pulled it to his ear. "Yeah?"

Walking to the window, he eased back the curtain and glanced down the long, dark driveway. The home was in the foothills, about thirty miles from town. Fairly isolated and supposedly safe.

Violet stretched to see out the window. Headlights appeared in the distance.

"Let him through," Clay said into the phone.

The vehicle moved forward.

Clay closed the cell. "Micah's here. He wants to talk to you."

She placed the mug on the coffee table and waited until the door opened and Micah stepped inside, stamping his boots on a small rug by the door. A swirl of frigid air entered with him.

He nodded to Violet, dropped his briefcase on the coffee table and shrugged out of his parka. "Storm's headed this way. Forecast is for snow and ice by tomorrow afternoon."

Hopefully by then, the murderer would have

been found, and Violet would be at the paper, finishing her next story.

"We've uncovered information about your informant," Micah said. "Gwyn Duncan was involved with a small-time mobster named Angelo Bertelli. From the motel records, she arrived in town four days ago."

"Gwyn came to Missoula, thinking I could help her escape Angelo and the mob." Violet's throat tightened. She'd done everything but help.

"Let's go over what happened."

Violet had relayed the information to Clay and again to the officer at the scene of the crime. For the third time, she recounted the story. Micah pulled a file from his briefcase and made notes on what she said.

When she finished, she looked at the two men. "That's it."

"What about your e-mail?" Micah asked.

"You can retrieve your messages, Violet, on my laptop." Clay booted up his computer and accessed the wireless Internet connection. She tapped in her e-mail account and password. Her inbox appeared with the messages from Gwyn.

Micah moved closer and read over Clay's shoulder. "Forward everything to my office computer so I can review them tomorrow."

"Got it. What about tonight's crime-scene photos?"

"I sent them to you as an attachment."

Clay opened the photos. The three of them huddled together and studied the pictures that flashed across the screen.

"Do you have Ruby Summers Maxwell's crime-scene photo?" Violet asked Micah.

He pulled a glossy 8x10 from his briefcase and handed it to her.

She stared at the picture. "Carlie's autopsy report mentioned—"

"How'd you get a copy of the report?" Clay's tone was sharp.

"A friend e-mailed it to me."

"A friend who's too free with classified information."

"Clay, please." Violet's head hurt, and she was too tired to think straight.

"We're all a little tense tonight," Micah said. "It's late and you're probably exhausted, Violet. I need a little more information. Jackson sent me the photo Clay took of Gwyn outside the coffee shop."

Violet was confused. "Why did Chicago FBI need her photo when she had left Chicago and was already in Montana?"

"You knew about the photo I took," Clay reminded her.

"But I thought Micah needed it, not the FBI. How freely does information pass around their Chicago office?"

Clay's eyes widened. "What are you implying?"

"That information about Gwyn could have gotten to the street. Wouldn't take long for Angelo to learn his girlfriend was hiding out in Missoula, Montana."

Violet rose from the couch still holding the crime-scene photo. All her attempts to protect her informant had failed. "I never should have told you anything about Gwyn. I trusted you, Clay. And Gwyn trusted me."

"Violet, you're overreacting." He stepped toward her.

She shook her head. "I told you too much, and you told your buddies everything. I learned cops couldn't be trusted long ago when they hauled my father into custody and interrogated him for hours. They wouldn't listen to the truth. They had their own agenda. Just like you, Clay. After what happened in Chicago, you needed to redeem yourself. If you brought down the mob, you'd be a hero."

"You know that's not true." Clay stepped toward her, but she backed up, knowing if he touched her she'd melt into his arms.

She had to remain strong. Too many women had died. Ruby and Carlie and now Gwyn.

What had she done wrong?

"You're not thinking rationally, Violet."

Her eyes teared. "Am I being stubborn? Like Aunt Lettie?" A huge lump lodged in her throat. "I tried to save her, but I couldn't."

His face softened. "Honey, what are you talking about?"

"I knew she was meeting her boyfriend that night when she put on the perfume he'd given her. She saved it for when they went out. My parents didn't know she'd snuck out of the house. The wind was howling through the trees. I ran after her, but it was dark, and I got scared." Tears ran down her cheeks.

"You were only seven, Violet."

"Don't you understand? I could have stopped her, but I got scared. If I hadn't run back home, Lettie would still be alive." Violet shook her head. "It was my fault that she died. That's why I need to find out if I did anything to cause Gwyn's death. Did I reveal something that led the mob to that motel? Maybe it was the information on my computer."

"We may never know how they tracked her down, but you can't blame yourself. The mob could have followed me to Missoula." Clay pointed to Micah. "Maybe someone in Billings learned Micah met with us. We can't know everything, Violet. Some things just happen. Sure we have to try to do better next time so no one else dies, but the mob doesn't play by the rules. That's why they have to be stopped."

No matter what Clay said, she couldn't move past the fact that something she'd done or said or written could have caused Gwyn's death.

She was shaking inside, the caffeine, the lack of sleep, the guilt she carried for Gwyn's murder. For Aunt Lettie's death.

Violet had fallen in love with Clay, relying on her heart instead of her head like a stupid schoolgirl. She'd thought too much about him and not enough about Gwyn's safety.

Violet ran from the living room. She stumbled into the bedroom, slammed the door and locked the latch behind her. Glancing down at Ruby's photo brought back the memory of Gwyn lying on the motel-room floor.

Violet threw herself on the bed and cried for all the women who had died—for Gwyn, for Carlie and Ruby and for Aunt Lettie, who had died so long ago.

She wanted to make everything turn out right. Instead, she'd brought more death and despair.

"Oh, God, I'm so sorry," she sobbed, her heart breaking. When would it end? The Mafia? The murders? The senseless destruction of human life?

Her own security no longer mattered. She had to warn other women in danger, like Jen Davis, who the Marshals couldn't find, and Olivia, who was on the run, as well as Eloise, the woman the mob wanted most of all.

Why hadn't she told Clay about the photo tacked on to the bulletin board at Mama's Diner? The marshals needed to know Olivia may have been a waitress there, yet Violet had withheld that information. She'd tell Clay about the photo when both of them had calmed down.

Right now, she wanted to concentrate on the three women who had died, so she could warn the other women still in danger. For their sakes, Violet had to publish the article on the mob, if it was the last thing she did.

Violet's words continued to circle through Clay's mind as he and Micah reviewed the information Violet had provided. Eventually Micah left, leaving Clay to wonder about his own role in tonight's murder.

Violet was right about one thing. Clay had passed on the information she'd provided to Jackson and Micah. But she had requested protection for Gwyn and had shared everything with Micah when they'd met at Police Headquarters.

Could there be a leak? Or was Clay imagining a problem where there wasn't one?

His cell rang.

"We found Ross Truett," Chief Howard said when Clay answered. "Pulled him in for questioning. The guy seems clean. He and Violet knew each other in college. He's doing a story on their alma mater for the *Yellowstone County Reader.* He called Violet a few days ago for a date. Dinner and a movie. Only she canceled on him today."

"What's he like?"

"Your average Joe. He's worried about her. Mentioned Jimmy Baker. Said the guy stayed a little too close to Violet in college. She'd landed an internship in Chicago. Jimmy had a hard time once she left town."

"Are you planning to talk to Jimmy?"

"We'll pull him in tomorrow. See if he knows anything. Why don't you come over in the morning? I'll fill you in on what we've come up with. I'd appreciate you taking an active role in this investigation. Might give you a chance to see how we do things in Missoula. Our department could use a fresh eye, especially someone with your experience."

Again, Clay appreciated the chief's support. "Sir, I'm still on probationary leave. The board hasn't made a decision yet."

"Jackson has full confidence in you. That's all I need."

"Thank you, sir."

Clay disconnected, then speed dialed Jackson's cell.

Although it was the middle of the night, he knew the agent wouldn't be sleeping.

"Thanks for putting in a good word for me with the Missoula chief of police," Clay said when Jackson answered.

"You know how I feel about what happened here in Chicago."

"If I hadn't lost my cool, we'd know the name of the head capo running the women on the street."

"We'll get to him, Clay. One way or another. No telling if he would have showed up that night or if he would have been exposed by the sting. We've been sure of a lot of things before, and they've fallen apart at the last second. These guys aren't known for stability. As you know, we want the men at the top. Vincent Martino and his father, Salvatore."

Clay heard the discouragement and fatigue in Jackson's voice. He'd been at this a long time. Fighting crime without seeing results took a toll. Clay knew that only too well.

"How's Violet?" the agent asked.

"Exhausted. She's trying to sleep."

Sadness settled over Clay when he disconnected. Gwyn had tried to make a difference. Violet had wanted to get her into Witness Protection. Now one woman was dead and the other felt responsible.

He dropped on to the couch. So much pain and despair. So many deaths. And law enforcement wasn't any closer to bringing down the Martino family.

Clay looked down the hallway to the door of the guest bedroom. Crazy to have thought he'd have a chance with Violet.

She deserved a good man who wasn't tainted

by the corruption that had surrounded Clay for too long. Violet needed a man who could love her *and* protect her.

Clay had thought he was that man. Now he knew better.

He glanced at the built-in bookcase. A small crystal cross like the ones he'd seen in gift-shop windows sat on the shelf.

Early on, Clay had questioned the reality of a God who could allow the bad things he saw every day on the streets of Chicago. Now he realized every man had a choice. He could choose good or evil. Trouble was, too many folks Clay came into contact with made bad decisions.

The book he'd read mentioned free will, a gift from God. The Lord couldn't interfere unless He was invited into a person's life. Clay glanced at the cross again, then flicked his eyes to Violet's door.

For more years than he wanted to admit, Clay had turned his back on God, claiming the Lord had been the one at fault. As a teen, he'd blamed God for his parents' deaths and then later for Sylvia's addiction. Everything was God's fault, when the real problem was Clay.

Violet had mixed up reality when she was seven and continued to hold on to the belief she could have saved her aunt if only Violet had followed her that night. In a similar way, Clay had mixed up the reality of his life. Accidents happened. Some people were prone to addiction. Others stole or killed to get what they wanted. But in spite of all the bad, God was good and loving and forgiving.

Lord, forgive me for the mistakes I've made, and if You need my invitation, so be it. Give me a hand here. Keep Violet safe. Help law enforcement find the person who killed Gwyn Duncan. Bring down the Martino family and every other arm of organized crime. Let good triumph over evil. Amen.

Clay felt an overwhelming sense of peace. Renewed by the prayer, he knew law enforcement would find Gwyn's killer and bring him to justice. Then Clay could leave Violet alone and let her get on with her life.

Reflecting on the choices a person could make, Clay realized leaving Violet would be the right choice for her, but the wrong choice for him.

SIXTEEN

Violet stayed awake throughout the night, trying to put the puzzle parts together. Was there anything she could have done that would have prevented Gwyn's death?

An intruder had entered Violet's home. Someone had gone into her files at work. More than likely the same person had stolen her laptop. Between the two computers, the intruder had accessed the information she had compiled on the Mafia. If the perpetrator had gotten into her e-mail, he would have seen the messages from Gwyn, as well.

Gwyn had run from the coffee shop, thinking someone from Chicago had been following Violet. Not Clay, but who?

Violet studied the photo of Ruby. As she had started to say to Clay earlier, Carlie's autopsy report mentioned a black smudge on the victim's right hand.

Looking closely at Ruby's photo, Violet realized her hand was similarly marked. The Mafia had been called the Black Hand in the early 1900s. Was the mob marking their victims?

Violet pulled up the photo she'd taken of Gwyn

on her cell. No such mark appeared on her hand. Maybe the Mafia hadn't killed Gwyn. If not, then who had committed the crime and why? Or had Violet surprised the killer before he'd had a chance to darken Gwyn's hand?

Footsteps sounded in the hallway followed by a knock at her door. "Violet, Chief Howard needs my help this morning."

Clay's voice.

"I'll be at Police Headquarters for a few hours."

She cracked the door open.

The gray light of another overcast day filtered through the hallway window. The subdued lighting played over Clay's face.

Unruly hair, heavy shadow of a beard and tired eyes reminded her of the way he'd looked that first night at the bar and grill in Chicago. Minus the cockiness.

But this morning, he was totally focused on his job. One hint of softening and she'd be in his arms. The pull between them had always been strong.

"Two guards are on the driveway," he stated matter-of-factly. "A couple more guys are in the woods. There's a radio on the coffee table. Push the squawk button to talk to them if you need anything."

Once again, he was a cop doing his job.

She searched his eyes, hoping he'd soften.

"Mrs. Jones and her husband just left for the

grocery store. They didn't expect company and need to stock up on supplies. She'll fix breakfast for you when she gets back."

"I'm not hungry." At least not for food. She was hungry for the old Clay to return. The man she'd fallen in love with who wrapped his arms around her when he walked her home, whose kiss sent her heart into freefall, who helped an older neighbor with odd jobs around the house because he was a good man who cared about others and wanted to make the world a better place.

"I'll have one of the guards come inside to stay with you," he said.

Violet didn't want anyone she didn't know underfoot. "No. Please don't."

"A female agent went to your home and packed a suitcase with everything you should need for the next few days."

"Twenty-four hours. No longer, Clay."

He held up his hands. "Violet, please, let me do my job for a change."

Her back bristled, recalling he'd said something similar last night. "For a change?"

"You didn't listen to me. I told you to stop investigating the mob. It almost cost you your life."

"Gwyn Duncan had to pay for my mistake. Is that what you're saying?"

He stretched out his right hand, palm up. "Give me your cell phone."

"What?"

"You can't call anyone today."

"I got the message last night."

"Promise?"

Now he was acting like a kid. "When I say I'll do something, I follow through, Clay." Not like cops who believed they were protecting the innocent then allowed killers to track down a woman on the run.

Anger bubbled up within her, anew. The Aunt Lettie side of her wanted to slam the door in his face.

She curbed the thought and instead asked a question that had troubled her all night. "Have they found Jen Davis yet?"

He shook his head ever so slightly.

"She's dead, isn't she?" Tears filled Violet's eyes. She blinked to keep them from spilling down her cheeks. She wouldn't let Clay see her cry again. Without waiting for his reply, she closed the door and turned the lock.

"Violet—"

Hot tears burned her cheeks.

"Violet, please."

Clay turned away from the door, and his footfalls sounded over the hardwoods, growing fainter and fainter. A door opened at the front of the house and closed forcefully. An engine revved to life. Tires rolled over the gravel drive.

Clay was leaving her, which was what he'd

planned all along. The FBI had wanted him to come to Missoula to quiet a nosy reporter. He'd done his job.

Her heart was breaking, but she shoved out her chin with determination. She had to go on even if Clay walked out of her life.

She followed the smell of coffee to the kitchen. After pouring a cup, she glanced out the window and spied a small dirt path on the far side of a dried creek bed.

Violet looked toward the front of the house. Two agents stood at the end of the driveway. A third man walked the woods in the rear. Another stood about thirty yards away.

Instead of feeling safe, she felt confined.

Wonder if they'd let her take a walk?

Probably against the rules.

She turned her back to the windows and leaned against the kitchen counter, sipping her coffee, drawing comfort from the warmth of the mug in her hands. Her gaze played over the round table, four ladder-back chairs and a computer sitting on a desk in the corner.

Violet pursed her lips. Clay hadn't said anything about checking her e-mail. She opened the computer and tapped in the address but found no new messages.

Force of habit, she then checked her old college Web site and was shocked when an e-mail appeared on the monitor screen.

You don't know me, but I have information about Lettie Kramer. I'm passing through Missoula. Meet me at Back Mountain Road at the five-mile turnoff so I can tell you what I know about your aunt.

She hit Reply.

What information do you have? Can you send it over the Web?

How could she get to Back Mountain Road? If she called Clay, he'd tell her she couldn't leave the safe house.

Glancing out the window, Violet spied the dirt path at the rear of the property. She knew the surrounding area. A few months back, she'd interviewed a woman who painted mountain scenes and lived close by. The staff photographer was sick that day, so Jimmy had gone with her and done the photo shoot.

A reply appeared in her in-box.

I have to give the information to you in person.

Violet needed to be careful, but this wasn't mob related, and it didn't involve the death of a green-eyed Montana woman. The mountain road wasn't far. She could get a cab at the nearby corner market she and Jimmy had stopped at and be back before anyone knew she was gone.

She pulled up a map of the area from the Internet. Just as she remembered, the dirt path out back led to one of the main roads. If she could think of some type of distraction, she might be able to slip away unnoticed. Noting the address of the next-door neighbor's house on the map, an idea took shape.

Violet found her suitcase in the living room and changed into a pair of jeans, warm sweater and hiking boots. Grabbing her coat and purse, she shut her bedroom door and left a note for the Joneses on the counter in the kitchen. *Rough night. I'm sleeping in. See you this afternoon.*

Glancing out the front window, she checked the driveway where the two agents were still standing. In the rear, the men were talking, their attention turned away from the thick band of spruce trees and pines surrounding the property.

Violet raised her cell and called 911. When the operator answered, Violet gave the neighbor's address and then said, "It looks like there's smoke in the woods."

Fire was always a problem during the dry periods, although usually not in winter. This year had proved the exception to the rule.

Violet hated to call in a false alarm. She mentally vowed to make a large donation to the fireman's association and beg forgiveness when this whole fiasco was over.

Sirens sounded in the distance. The two agents in front turned their attention to the approaching fire trucks.

An agent in the rear circled to the front of the house and watched the engines pull to a stop at the neighbor's house. The other man kept his focus on the firemen scurrying into the woods.

Violet slipped from the house. If she could make it to the protection of the thick wall of evergreens, she might be able to get away unnoticed.

A car turned into the driveway and stopped. The older couple who lived in the safe house climbed out. Mr. Jones said something, then pointed toward the neighbor's property. Mrs. Jones held her hand over her eyes as if to block the winter glare.

Violet pushed into the dense thicket. Evergreens folded around her. The lone rear agent glanced at where she stood, heart pounding in her chest. He took a step forward.

One of the men in front called out to him. "Looks like a false alarm."

The guy waved his arm in the air, signaling he'd heard. His attention broken, he turned and walked to the other side of the property.

Letting out a sigh of relief, Violet wove deeper into the pines, heading for the main road that would take her to the corner market.

She'd walked less than ten minutes when her

cell rang. Violet looked at the caller ID and hit the talk button.

"I've been a jerk." Jimmy's voice. "I'm sorry, Violet. I had this stupid notion that something could develop between us. Finally I had a little heart to heart with myself."

She smiled at the mental picture.

"Stu's mad you didn't call in today," he added.

"I'll phone him as soon as I can."

"What's going on?"

"I can't tell you anything, Jimmy."

"It involves that cop, doesn't it? I called your home last night, but no one answered. I want to help you. After all, we've been friends for a long time."

As much as Violet didn't want to involve anyone else, she did need help. "I have to meet someone at Back Mountain Road. He—or she—has information about my aunt Lettie. I don't have a car so I'll have to call a cab. Do you have the number for the cab company?"

"Forget the cab. I'll pick you up at your house."

But she wasn't home.

And she didn't want to get him involved. Clay would go through the roof if he found out Jimmy had helped her, but Clay was at Police Headquarters and she had a problem that needed to be solved.

"Remember that photo shoot we did on the mountain artist? Could you meet me in front of the corner market where we bought ice cream bars that day? It's at the junction of Hawkins and Summit."

"Yeah, I remember. In fact, I'm not far from there now. Stu wants me to cover a human-interest piece out that way. I've got an interview in fifteen minutes. I can call the lady and tell her I'll have to reschedule for later. But, Violet, what are you doing so far from town?"

"I'll tell you when I see you."

"Give me ten minutes."

With Jimmy's help, Violet would be able to get the information concerning Aunt Lettie. Information she needed to clear her father's name. Information that could signal the end of a mystery, which had plagued her family for too long.

Violet should feel elated.

Instead, she was upset she had to go behind Clay's back.

SEVENTEEN

Micah arrived at Police Headquarters shortly after Clay. Together, they drove back to the scene of the murder, looking for anything that might have been missed last night. A thorough search of the motel room and surrounding area revealed nothing new.

Returning to headquarters, Clay phoned Violet, but the call went to voice mail. He had told her not to talk to anyone on her cell. Knowing Violet, she probably realized the call was from him and had folded her arms over her chest and cocked her hip with a but-you-told-me-not-to-use-my-phone attitude.

"Ah, Violet, you are too much." A smile twitched his lips. He'd never take her for granted. She always had something new up her sleeve.

Chuckling, he called the safe house. Mrs. Jones answered.

"Could you put Violet on the line?"

"She's sleeping in, Clay. Catching up on the rest she missed last night."

He glanced at his watch. Almost 10:00 a.m. Pouting in her room was probably more accurate.

He'd check on the guards to ensure everything was going smoothly.

"Any problems?" Clay asked when the agent in charge answered.

"None at this house."

"Meaning—?"

"Someone called in a fire alarm down the road. Two engines answered the call. They couldn't find the fire or the person who phoned 911."

"Has anyone checked on Ms. Kramer?"

"She's sleeping, sir."

Clay's hand gripped his cell. He spoke slowly and distinctly. "Ensure she's still inside."

The radio squawked as one of the rear guards checked the house before the answer came back. "Ms. Kramer is not in the house, sir."

"Find her," Clay ordered. "Canvass the property and surrounding area. Check with the neighbors. See if anyone saw a vehicle about the time of the fire alarm. Somebody must have seen something."

Clay passed the information on to the chief.

"I'll dispatch every officer I can spare to search for her."

"What about Jimmy Baker?" Clay asked. "Have you hauled him in for questioning?"

"He's out on a story but due back at the paper by early afternoon. We'll pick him up then."

Clay would feel better once that loose cannon

was interrogated. "What about the other people on staff?"

"Like who?" the chief asked.

Clay sighed. "Forget it. I'll call the editor."

But before he called Stu, he needed to tell Jackson what had happened. Clay left the chief's office and moved into a vacant conference room to place the call.

"Where would she go?" the agent asked after Clay explained the situation.

"Knowing Violet, back to The *Daily News*. Have you had time to run a check on the staff at the *Daily News*?"

"The only one with an Illinois connection was Quinn Smith. He grew up in Chicago. I don't know when he moved West, but he's been at the Missoula paper for some time."

"Would you mind circulating Quinn's name on the street? Doubt we'll get lucky, but you never know."

"I'm heading out for a little *tête-à-tête* with Cameron Trimble. I'll run the name by him. If there's anything to learn about Quinn, we'll get it for you."

"Thanks, Jackson."

"Listen, Clay, I need to ask. If Cameron comes forward with anything, he may want to plea bargain. After what he did to Sylvia . . . ?" Jackson paused. "It's your call."

For so long, Clay had wanted to make Cameron

pay for what he'd done to his ex-wife. Now, with Violet in danger, vengeance didn't seem so sweet. Clay couldn't forgive Cameron, at least not yet, but he would agree to a plea bargain. "If he's got information to share, do whatever it takes."

Once he disconnected, Clay plugged in the editor's number.

"What's going on?" Stu asked when he got on the line. "The police were here earlier, looking for Jimmy. Violet never showed up for work. Is she in trouble?"

"Have you heard from her?"

"Not this morning."

"What about the others on staff?"

"Quinn hasn't shown up, either."

Chief Howard stepped from his office, phone pressed against his ear, and motioned to Clay.

"Hold on, Stu." Clay approached the chief. "Yes, sir?"

"One of the neighbors saw a woman matching Violet's description get into a car outside a country market about half a mile from the safe house."

"Did the person know the make and model?"

"This gal's the type of citizen a cop likes. She copied down the license. We ran a check. The car belongs to Jimmy Baker."

Clay pulled his cell back to his ear. "Stu, tell me everything you know about Jimmy Baker, starting with his home address."

• • •

Driving toward Back Mountain Road, Violet filled Jimmy in on the basics. A woman had died. Violet had found her body and was being kept in protective custody for her own safety.

The e-mail today had been an unexpected surprise. A person passing through Missoula had information about Lettie and wanted to talk to Violet.

The mountain road intersected with Interstate 90 that ran from Spokane to Missoula to Chicago and on to the East Coast. The person had probably looked at a map for a private spot to meet not far from the highway.

The turnoff on Back Mountain Road lay just ahead.

Violet's cell rang. She glanced at the caller ID. Clay West.

She couldn't talk to him now. Clay would say she'd acted irresponsibly, first by calling in a false fire alarm and then by eluding the guards who were working hard to protect her.

In her mind's eye, she saw his furrowed brow, dark eyes and look of disappointment that she would have done something so terribly foolish. Later, when she had the information about Lettie, she'd call him back and beg his forgiveness.

As soon as Gwyn's murderer was apprehended, Clay would leave Montana and head home to

Chicago. No reason for him to hang around any longer.

She glanced at Jimmy. He'd always been there to help her out. "I'm sorry I got you into this," she said as he turned into the clearing.

"And I'm sorry I acted like a fool. I've been jealous of that cop from Chicago. The way he looks at you, I knew there was something going on between you. Something special."

Maybe there had been at one time, but things had changed. Violet had to steel her heart to the reality that she and Clay didn't have a future together. He was a cop who had a job to do in Chicago. She would stay in Missoula to help where she could here.

Jimmy braked to a stop.

An SUV sat parked in the distance. Slowly, it eased forward. Tinted windows made it impossible for her to see the driver.

The vehicle pulled next to them and stopped. When the driver climbed out, Violet was more confused than ever. She opened the door and stepped on to the pavement. "I didn't expect to see you here."

She saw the knife in his hand, realizing too late she'd made a deadly mistake.

Clay arrived at Jimmy's house ahead of the three squad cars. He parked down the street and made his way through the rear of the property to the back porch. He wanted to crash through the door and grab Jimmy, but he needed to be cautious. He couldn't do anything that would cause Violet harm.

If Jimmy hurt her, Clay would show him no mercy.

Two Missoula cops sidled around the corner of the house, headed for the front door. Two more officers joined Clay on the back porch, weapons drawn. His fingers itched for the service revolver under lock and key back at Chicago P.D. Being unarmed was one of the complications of administrative leave.

Clay nodded to the officers and opened the door. He slipped inside, silent as a cat, glancing right then left. Dining room straight ahead, living area beyond. The front door opened, and two officers entered, guns raised. One man headed for the back bedrooms. A second man moved to the basement door and slipped into the darkness below.

Clay was drawn into the main room like a moth to flame. Oriental rug spread in front of a stone fireplace. Leather couch and love seat. Glass coffee table. In the blink of an eye, he took it all in.

His eyes turned to study the walls covered with framed photographs. A heavy dread settled over his shoulders.

The person captured in each picture was Violet Kramer.

EIGHTEEN

Violet tried to scream, but the rag stuffed in her mouth and held in place with duct tape kept any sound from escaping.

She saw the top of his head in the driver's seat. Hooded sweatshirt. Baseball cap.

Back at the clearing, he'd shoved Jimmy's car over the drop-off with Jimmy in it. When she'd struggled, he'd struck her face, knocking her out. She'd come to bound and gagged and lying on the backseat of his SUV. Her head was jammed against the door handle.

She tried to get her bearings. All she could see out of the passenger window was the overhead cloud cover and gray sky. She blinked against the glare and struggled to rise off the seat.

The sound of the tires hummed along the pavement. The driver decelerated, easing the car into a turn. Using her elbow as a prop, she inched up, her eyes even with the window. Straining, she pulled up even more and glanced down.

Her stomach roiled.

The world shifted.

Chest tight, she couldn't breathe.

The car was racing along the mountain road

just inches from a steep drop-off. Far below, she saw a tiny village nestled in the valley.

A moan rose from within her. One slip of the tires, and they would hurl down the side of the cliff and crash on to the craggy rocks below.

Clay stared at the photographs of Violet. Many of the shots appeared to be taken without her knowledge. Some were of a younger Violet, holding books in her arms.

Jimmy had been obsessed with her since college.

Now he had her.

The cops were combing the city.

Clay looked at her beautiful eyes and smiling face. The curls and curves and exquisite smile were all he'd ever wanted. If only he could spend the rest of his life holding her in his arms.

Oh, God, help me. Clay raked his hands through his short hair. He had to find her. Had to find her alive.

Lord, I've turned my back on You for so many years, but if You are a loving God, give me a break. Provide a clue that leads to Violet.

One of the officers stepped into the living room, a cell phone pressed to his ear. "Yes, sir. We've searched the house but didn't find anything or anyone." He paused. "He's right here."

The cop held out the cell to Clay. "Chief Howard wants to talk to you."

Clay took the phone. "Sir?"

"We found Jimmy's car. Went over the turn-around on a mountain road."

"Violet?"

"She wasn't in the car."

"What about Jimmy?"

"Survived the forty-foot drop. He's in bad shape but alive. They're taking him into surgery."

"Did he say anything?"

"He was unconscious, Clay."

"Maybe Violet wasn't with him." Perhaps this had all been a terrible bad dream.

"We found her cell phone in the front seat."

"Could she have survived the fall and gotten out? Maybe she's wandering along some mountain path?"

"I've got a team searching the area."

"Give me directions. I want to help."

"The weather's changing, Clay. A storm's rolling in. Let my men handle it."

"Chief, please. You said you could use me."

His plea worked. The chief gave Clay directions. The mountain road wasn't far from the safe house.

Clay covered the distance in record time. Violet could be wandering around the mountain injured. Temperatures were dropping. The wind had increased, and from the looks of the gray sky, Mother Nature was about to do her thing.

As he drove up the side of the mountain, a light

drizzle began to fall. The precipitation increased with the elevation. By the time Clay pulled into the clearing, the rain had turned to sleet that froze against his windshield.

If Violet was in those open-toe heels she always wore and her cute lightweight coat without a hat or mittens, she'd freeze to death. He had to find her.

An ominous sense of dread settled over him. Violet was good and pure and innocent. She didn't deserve to be sucked into this terrible situation.

Had he been the reason? If he'd said no to Jackson and stayed in Chicago maybe none of this would have happened. He'd interfered and tried to solve everything his own way. Once again, it hadn't worked.

He glanced at the darkening sky, feeling the cold penetrate the car. He shoved the defroster to high to clear the ice from the windshield, but even the wipers couldn't keep up with the heavy winter mix.

The wheels slipped in the freezing slush.

Nearing the turnaround, his cell rang.

He flipped it open.

Jackson's voice. The words were tumbling out one after another. "Cameron spilled the beans on a guy who used to be a regular in some of the clubs the mob ran in Chicago. Thought he was a high roller. Got used to the nightlife but gambled away everything he had in savings. Said he'd make good on the rest of it. Not too long ago, the mob pulled in the chips. Told him to take care of a little problem in Missoula and they'd call it even. I notified Chief Howard. He sent a patrol car to the guy's house, but he'd cleared out."

"Yeah?"

"He's got a cabin. Higher elevation. At the summit of Dead Man's Peak."

"Are you talking about Gwyn's boyfriend?"

"No, the other guy you mentioned. The reporter from the *Daily News.*"

Clay tensed. "You mean, Jimmy?"

"No. I'm talking about Quinn Smith."

NINETEEN

Violet's eyes opened when the SUV stopped. She moaned. Everything was starting to come back to her in bits and pieces.

Jimmy had struggled to protect her from Quinn. The two men had fought. Quinn knocked Jimmy out then shoved him back into his car. She'd tried to stop Quinn, but he'd raised his hand and struck her. The last thing she remembered was Jimmy's car, with him in it, crashing over the edge of the steep drop-off.

Violet had blacked out and awakened crumpled in the backseat until her glance out the window had slammed her into darkness again. She blinked and tried to get her bearings.

The wind howled and icy snow hurled against the windshield. A small shack sat huddled against the edge of the mountain.

The car door opened. Quinn grabbed her arm and yanked her from the backseat. Her foot caught on the door. She fell, crashing to the frigid ground.

He jerked her upright. She looked toward the edge of the cliff. Her head swam and her stomach roiled.

She gagged.

He ripped the tape from her face and pulled the wad of fabric from her mouth. She retched again.

Thrashing against his arms, she tried to get free. He caught her hands, his grip as strong as a vise.

"Control yourself, Violet."

Snow and sleet stung her face. "You're a madman," she screamed into the wind. Her hair swirled around her face.

He pinned her against his hip and shoved her around the car.

"You never had information about my aunt."

"No, but I saw your Web site and knew you'd do anything to learn how she'd died. Even meet me on the edge of the mountain."

"What do you want from me?" Violet demanded.

"I want your boyfriend. Someone needs to teach him a lesson."

"You killed Gwyn."

"I had to. She recognized me and knew I had ties to the mob."

Violet tried to make sense of everything that had happened. "You followed me to the coffee shop."

"The mob told me to get rid of you. But I wanted to give you a chance, Violet. That's why I tried to scare you. Fool that you are, you didn't take the hint."

"You were the man standing in my kitchen, and you deleted my files at work. Did you steal my home laptop, as well?" She knew the answer before he spoke. "How'd you get into my house?"

Once again she realized her error. "You lifted my keys from my purse when I was at work. Easy enough to make a wax impression and have a new one made from the mold."

"Now you're thinking like the mob, Violet. I'm sorry you could never write that story you wanted. I'll write one, talking about how a bad cop from Chicago, who had beaten a guy almost to death, played up to you. Jimmy tried to save you but died when he went over the edge of the turnaround. Clay pulled you into his car. He thought the mountain road intersected with Highway 90. The weather was bad and his car— with you in it—skidded into the mountain and went up in flames. I'll torch Clay's car with both of you in it so the police will buy the story."

The man was deranged. "You won't get away with it, Quinn."

"I know the cops. I'll explain how Clay had been jealous of Jimmy. Clay brought you up the mountain, never realizing it was a dead end at the top."

Quinn moved her closer to the edge. "Maybe I should shove you over now and get rid of you that way. Then I'll wait out here for Clay and handle him when he gets here. The mob wants him out of the picture. He got too close in Chicago, throwing his weight around, beating up one of their men, infiltrating their operation."

Her head swam. Her knees went weak. She had to fight to save herself, but Quinn held her in a death grip.

She screamed as the ledge crumbled underfoot.

Clay clutched the steering wheel, white knuckled. The back tires skidded dangerously close to the edge of the road that dropped off into oblivion.

The steep mountain peak loomed above him. Quinn would be waiting at the top. Would Violet still be alive?

Clay had to get to her in time.

The temperature plummeted with the increased elevation, freezing everything into a sheet of ice. Up ahead, Clay watched as a portion of the road broke off and slid down the mountain, leaving only a tiny edge too narrow for a car to navigate.

Clay braked to a stop and forced the door open against the wind. He'd have to travel the last hundred yards on foot.

Oh, God, help me. Let me get to Violet while she's still alive.

He blinked against the sleet that fell like shards of ice and froze to his face, chapping his lips and stinging his cheeks.

He glanced ahead.

One last switchback. The cabin was perched

around the final turn where he'd find Quinn.

The only way to surprise him would be to leave the path and climb up the rocky side of the mountain. Approaching from the rear, Clay might be able to get a drop on him.

Clay grabbed the rough rock, found a foothold and hoisted himself up, then searched for another crevice so he could climb higher.

He glanced down the sheer drop-off. Vertigo rolled over him, throwing his equilibrium into a tailspin. He clutched the rock until it passed.

Wind whipped around him. The frozen stone numbed his hands. He started out again, gaining a foothold, then another. Inch by inch, he crawled to the top and hoisted himself over a final cluster of boulders. Flattening himself against the side of the small hovel, Clay peered around the corner.

His heart dropped.

Quinn held Violet around the waist while her legs dangled over the edge of the mountain.

Violet screamed. Quinn stepped back. Her feet touched ground again. She almost fainted with relief. He laughed and pulled a hunting knife from the sheath on his belt.

Her heart stopped. She had to get away.

"Quinn?"

Clay's voice. He stood at the side of the cabin.

"Watch out!" she screamed. "He's got a knife."

With one arm around her chest, Quinn pressed the razor-sharp blade to her throat, nicking her flesh. Drops of blood trickled down her neck.

She struggled, trying to get away.

"Let her go." Clay raised his hands and stepped forward. "Take me instead, Quinn. I'm not armed. I can't hurt you."

"You don't understand," Quinn said. "I have to kill her."

"It has to do with your gambling debts, doesn't it?" Clay's voice was calm.

"They told me the slate would be wiped clean if I got rid of Violet."

She shivered from the biting cold and raw fear that made her gasp for air.

"Cameron's back in Chicago," Clay said. "He told the cops about you."

"You're lying."

"They'll find you, Quinn. Jimmy's alive, but only barely. If he dies, you'll get Murder One."

Clay glanced at Violet. His eyes conveyed strength and determination. "Let her go and it'll be easier for you."

Quinn sneered. "You're trying to fool me."

He took a step back, dragging Violet along with him. She looked down. Another few inches and they'd both tumble over the edge.

"Violet?" Clay's voice was reassuring. Instinctively, she knew what he wanted her to do.

Somehow, she had to distract Quinn. But she couldn't. She was too frightened.

She needed Clay. She'd always needed him.

"Help me," she whimpered.

"Remember we're a team," he said with conviction.

A team meant she did her part and Clay would do his. For once, everything didn't rest on her shoulders. She didn't have to be totally in control.

Quinn's hands shook. The cold was affecting him. He glanced over his shoulder.

Violet shoved her weight against him.

He lost his balance. The knife dropped through his fingers, and his hold on her eased ever so slightly.

She swiveled out of his grasp then started to fall. Clay grabbed her hand and pulled her to safety.

Quinn's arms flailed.

Clay lunged for him. The two locked grips before Quinn slipped over the edge. His legs pedaled the air. A cross draft caught him, ripping his hand free.

Throwing himself down on to the frozen ground, Clay grabbed Quinn's coat, catching him just in time.

The weight pulled Clay forward.

Violet screamed, slapping at Clay's leg, trying to stop the fateful fall.

His foot locked around a boulder.

Straining, Clay dragged Quinn up and over the edge.

Violet reached for the discarded knife and shoved it into Clay's hand. Holding the blade to Quinn's neck, Clay forced him to turn over then tied the reporter's arms behind him, using his own belt. Once Quinn was secure, Clay pulled Violet into his arms.

She trembled in his embrace. The terrible nightmare was over. She'd almost lost Clay. Nothing had terrified her more.

Far below, shouts from the police sounded.

"We're up here," Clay yelled. "Everything's under control."

Violet heard Clay's heart beat in sync with hers. Wrapped in his warmth, she felt life flowing back into her trembling body. The mountain, the ice, the cliff, nothing mattered except being in Clay's arms.

TWENTY

Two weeks later, Violet and Clay stood in the dining room of Bernice's house. The endearing neighbor busied herself in the kitchen, while Violet arranged a bouquet of red roses Clay had given her in a crystal vase.

"They're beautiful, Clay."

"Not as beautiful as you."

Violet smiled as she placed the arrangement in the center of the dining-room table. Grabbing a pitcher from the sideboard, she filled the water glasses at each of the six place settings.

"Are you sure we can't help you?" Clay called to Bernice in the kitchen.

"Everything's almost ready. You and Violet visit in the living room. Leonard should arrive in the next few minutes. Watch for him while I take off this apron and put on some lipstick."

"Micah phoned. He picked Jade up from that librarian's workshop she attended on campus today. They'll be here soon. Thanks for including them tonight, Bernice."

"The more the merrier." She stepped into the hallway, heading for her bedroom.

"How'd the meeting go at Police Headquarters?" Violet asked Clay once the two of them were alone.

"I told Chief Howard I'd accept the position with the Missoula P.D., if and when the problem in Chicago is resolved."

"You haven't heard anything?"

"Not yet. I thought they'd make their announcement by now. But I do have news that will interest you."

She slipped her hand into his, eager to hear what he had to say.

"Cameron has been talking to the FBI. Do you remember Lettie's boyfriend?"

"Brad Meyers. Of course I do."

"I asked Jackson if he could find out anything about him. Turns out the FBI pulled a guy off the street who knew Brad in Detroit. The guy said alcohol loosened Brad's tongue one night, and he bragged about killing a high school student and a gal who had been in love with him."

Tears sprung to Violet's eyes.

"They haven't found him yet, but I'm positive once they do, your father's name will finally be cleared."

"Thank you," she whispered, dabbing her eyes and trying to control the overwhelming gratitude that flowed through her. Clay kissed her cheek, which caused her to smile. "What about Cameron? Did he provide anything that could be used against the Martino family?" she asked.

"Not per se, but he did expose the guy who runs most of the prostitution on the South side. It's not the capo, but this guy's big enough. Chicago law enforcement will be able to clean up at least part of the city. They're trying to help the women who want a new start in life."

"That's good news," Violet said. "Stu got a call from Jimmy today. He's improving physically and agreed to long-term psychiatric care."

Clay squeezed her hand. "I know you worry about him."

"I feel responsible."

"Honey, he was obsessed with you. That's not your fault. It'll take time, but hopefully, intensive therapy will straighten him out."

Violet knew Clay was right, but she still worried about Jimmy. There was someone else she worried about, as well. "Did Micah mention Jen Davis?"

"Only that they located a woman who matches her description. She goes by the name of Hannah Shore. They're keeping her under surveillance."

"Olivia and Eloise?"

Clay shook his head. "No news yet."

Before Clay could say anything else, his cell rang. He glanced at the caller's name and smiled as he flipped it open.

"Hey, Jackson. How's everything in Chicago?"

Clay's face grew serious as they talked. Finally,

he grinned. "Thanks. Yeah, she's right here. I'll put her on."

Violet took the phone.

"Clay said you came to a decision about the Mafia story," Jackson said.

"I decided to sit on it. I won't print anything about the mob or the Martino family or the women who were killed until I hear from you."

"Thanks, Violet. You'll get an exclusive when it's all over," Jackson said. "I can promise you that."

"But I would like to write a piece on Gwyn Duncan, if that's okay. I'll send you a copy of the story to get your approval before it goes to print."

"No need to get my approval. I trust your good judgment. Enjoy your dinner tonight, and tell my brother and future sister-in-law I said hello."

Violet handed the phone back to Clay. He looked like a helium balloon ready to explode.

"Do you have some news to share?" she asked once he had pocketed his cell phone.

"The inquiry voted in my favor. Chicago P.D. learned more from Cameron than they would have in the sting we had planned. Jackson said they found me completely in the clear."

"Oh, Clay, that's wonderful."

"Better than that, it means I can accept the job here in Missoula. You'll have me underfoot. Bernice will be happy."

"Having you underfoot is exactly where I want you, too." Violet laughed. He still had eyes a woman could get lost in, and his aftershave made her heart race. "I called my parents and told them there's someone I want them to meet."

"You did?"

"I told them we make a good team."

"Did you mention we finally learned how to work together?"

Hopefully, her smile didn't reveal what she'd really told her parents—that she'd found Mr. Right, the man she wanted to team up with for the rest of her life.

A car door slammed, and Violet glanced out the window. Clay stood at her side, his arm around her shoulders. Together they watched Micah open the passenger door and help Jade Summers, a beautiful redhead, as she stepped on to the sidewalk.

Thanks to Bernice's warm hospitality, Clay and Violet would get to know Jade over dinner tonight. The two couples would visit again tomorrow after church before Micah and Jade drove back to Billings.

As they walked toward the house, Violet turned to face Clay. His arms circled her waist.

"You were right, Clay."

He raised his brow.

"About the Mafia," she continued. "You warned me, but I was too . . . "

"Too Aunt Lettie?" he suggested.

Violet laughed. "My mother is going to love you."

His mood sobered. "And what about you, Violet? Any chance you could fall in love with a cop from Chicago?"

As much as she enjoyed bantering with words, sometimes actions spoke louder. She wrapped her arms around his neck and drew him even closer.

Their lips met, and everything she'd ever wanted was wrapped in the magic of that moment. Violet didn't need the big story or the killer headline, God had brought Clay into her life and nothing else mattered. Then just to be sure he got the message, she pulled back ever so slightly.

"Do I love you?" Violet whispered. "The answer is yes."

Dear Reader,

Thanks for reading *Killer Headline*, the second book in the Protecting the Witnesses continuity series. The series features heroic men and memorable women whose lives are changed because of the Witness Protection Program. In six very special stories, good triumphs over evil, God's transforming love brings forgiveness and healing and distant hearts are united forever.

In my story, newspaper reporter Violet Kramer learns self-reliance must be tempered with a willingness to accept the help of others. Most especially, she needs to accept God's help. Officer Clay West sees firsthand how God can bring good from pain and suffering, but he must forgive those who have wronged him in the past before he can fully accept the love of the Lord. If you have trouble accepting help or if you've been hurt by others, turn to God, who is the source of all strength.

I'd love to hear from you. E-mail me at debby@debbygiusti.com or write to me c/o Steeple Hill, 233 Broadway, Suite 1001, New York, NY 10279. To learn about my next Love

Inspired Suspense, visit me online at www.DebbyGiusti.com.

May your life be enriched by the books you read.

Wishing you abundant blessings,

QUESTIONS FOR DISCUSSION

1. Violet knows her strength is writing hard-hitting stories, but she's impetuous and pushes too hard. How does the editor teach Violet patience?

2. What is the real reason Violet didn't land a permanent position on the *Chicago Gazette*? What could she have done differently?

3. The seeds of faith Eloise planted in Clay so long ago eventually bear fruit. Have you been discouraged when those you love closed their hearts to the Lord? If the seeds you planted seemed to fall on rocky or sandy soil, did you lose heart? What do you need to remember about God's love and mercy?

4. What caused the fight between Clay and Cameron? What did Clay learn about himself? How did the fight affect him?

5. Why did Violet go into journalism? What does she hope to accomplish? What does she learn over the course of this story?

6. Bernice showers Clay with affirmation and praise. How does he respond? What can you learn from Bernice's example?

7. Self-reliance is admirable to a certain point. Explain why Violet needs to sometimes accept help from others.

8. Was Violet wrong to call in the false fire alarm? Does the end ever justify the means?

9. After reading about the father who forgave his daughter's murderer, Clay reflected on his own life. What conclusions did he come to and whom does he need to forgive?

10. How did the pain in Clay's past affect his life? Do you know someone who has been wounded? How can you reach out to them with love?

11. Growing up in Granite Pass, Violet was a loner and felt isolated from her peers. Was it their rejection or the wall she built around herself that closed Violet out?

12. Violet has been unsuccessful in finding information about Aunt Lettie's murder. What does she finally do? Will Violet be able to forgive the killer when he is brought to justice?

13. Clay had listened to Eloise in the foster home when she talked about the Lord. What events caused him to turn away from God? Would his life have been different if he had drawn closer to God instead? What had to happen before he could accept the Lord into his life again?

14. Does Violet have a close relationship with her father? What brought you to that conclusion?

15. The book about the father's forgiveness touched Clay. Which books have impacted your life? Can God use the written word—even fictional tales—to teach His people? What criteria do you use in choosing a good book to read?

DEBBY GIUSTI is a medical technologist who loves working with test tubes and petri dishes almost as much as she loves to write. Growing up as an army brat, Debby met and married her husband—then a captain in the army—at Fort Knox, Kentucky. Together they traveled the world, raised three wonderful army brats of their own and have now settled in Atlanta, Georgia, where Debby spins tales of suspense that touch the heart and soul. Contact Debby through her Web site, www.DebbyGiusti.com, e-mail debby@debbygiusti.com, or write c/o Steeple Hill, 233 Broadway, Suite 1001, New York, NY 10279.

Center Point Publishing
600 Brooks Road • PO Box 1
Thorndike ME 04986-0001 USA

(207) 568-3717

US & Canada:
1 800 929-9108
www.centerpointlargeprint.com